E. Augusta King

The Diary of a Civilian's Wife in India, 1877-1882

Vol. I.

E. Augusta King

The Diary of a Civilian's Wife in India, 1877-1882
Vol. I.

ISBN/EAN: 9783337017781

Printed in Europe, USA, Canada, Australia, Japan

Cover: Foto ©Andreas Hilbeck / pixelio.de

More available books at **www.hansebooks.com**

THE DIARY

OF

A CIVILIAN'S WIFE IN INDIA

1877—1882

BY

MRS ROBERT MOSS KING

Tis pleasant, sure, to see one's name in print;
A book 's a book although there 's nothing in 't'
BYRON

'I have no other but a woman's reason;
I think him so—because I think him so'
SHAKSPERE

WITH NUMEROUS ILLUSTRATIONS

IN TWO VOLUMES—VOL. I.

LONDON

RICHARD BENTLEY & SON, NEW BURLINGTON STREET

Publishers in Ordinary to Her Majesty the Queen

1884

TO

MY SISTER

WITHOUT WHOSE LOVING SYMPATHY AND NEVER-FAILING INTEREST

THIS DIARY WOULD NEVER HAVE BEEN WRITTEN

AND TO

MY CHILDREN

THIS RECORD OF FIVE HAPPY YEARS

IS

Affectionately Dedicated

PREFACE.

THIS DIARY was written without any idea that it would ever be read beyond the circle of my own family, and, being written from day to day and without any possibility of after-correction (being sent home every few weeks), it has no doubt often the inaccuracy and one-sidedness of first impressions.

As a plain daily record, however, of the life led by most Englishwomen in the North of India, it is hoped it may interest those who have a sister or daughter whose married life is cast, as mine was, in India.

I should be glad if it brought a truer picture of the daily interests and trials of Indian life before those who are apt to think of it as being all fun and gaiety, or, on the other hand, a mixture of snakes, heat, and dulness—flat and unprofitable.

Such as it is, I commend it to the good nature of my possible readers and critics, with the hope that they will be—

> To its merits very kind,
> To its faults—a little blind.

CONTENTS

OF

THE FIRST VOLUME.

————◦❖◦————

CHAPTER VI.

CHAPTER VII.

CHAPTER VIII.

CHAPTER IX.

CHAPTER X.

CHAPTER XI.

CHAPTER XII.

CHAPTER XIII.

CHAPTER XIV.

CHAPTER XV.

ILLUSTRATIONS

TO

THE FIRST VOLUME.

———◆———

A CIVILIAN'S WIFE IN INDIA.

CHAPTER I.

IN THE RED SEA—AUSTRIAN LLOYD'S STEAMER—PILGRIMS
FOR MECCA—JEDDAH—EVE'S TOMB—SLAVERY.

Nov. 4, 1877.—' The sun's perpendicular rays
illumine the depths of the sea,' and we are in
like case with the fishes, and wish that like them
we had nothing but scales on. Up till now we
have had nothing to complain of, having had
charming weather ever since leaving Trieste.
The weather was cold at first, and grew steadily
warmer every day, until the thermometer stands
at 90° in the shade as I write. We are only $6\frac{1}{2}$
cabin passengers in all : our two selves, two
German men of business, a German Frau with
a little boy of six (he is the half-passenger), who

confided to me that his father lived at Cawnpore and sold boots, and an Irish girl just returning to India after spending two years in Germany. She takes daily lessons in the zither from the third officer on board, a pleasant, cheery young Austrian.

The passengers are not a conversational set ; we sometimes go and have a chat with the Chief Engineer, an Englishman, whose ideas seem strictly limited to engines. We ask him concerning the ship's course, the currents, and so on, but his invariable answer is that he does not know much about those things, so we fall back on engines, revolutions, and screws. At dinner we talk to the Captain, who speaks French fluently, though German is his native tongue ; he has some grievance with the Directors of the Company at Trieste, and gets so excited over their conduct that he forgets to eat his dinner, and sorely tries the patience of the stewards, who are longing to clear away the table. The poor old Captain says he has spent his whole life *en lutte* with his superiors, and his chief consolation lies in recounting how he confronts the Board of Directors and says, 'Messieurs! vous êtes des voleurs! des canailles!!' One can imagine this does not oil the wheels of their intercourse.

At Port Said we took on board 400 pilgrims from Syria, Palestine, and the coasts, bound for Mecca. It was very amusing watching them come on board and shake down as best they could. A passage running round the dining-saloon was put apart for the women and children, where they squatted down with their water-bottles and baskets of fruit and provisions for the journey, and where they stayed patiently for a whole week, as patient and well-behaved as the same number of cattle would have been. The male pilgrims arranged themselves and their bundles all over the deck, few of them having enough room to lie out at full length. We thought the ship was as full as it could be, till we reached Suez, when we were told to prepare for another 150 pilgrims! I did not see how it was possible to provide standing room for them, but as boat after boat full of them arrived, and they swarmed up on deck like so many ants, the scene became even more confused and hopeless than I had imagined. They were forced on deck by the weight of those crowding after, but there they stuck in a solid writhing mass, some struggling vainly in one direction, some in another. A few poor women simply succumbed, and sat down to let fate do its worst. I suppose they were of Tristram Shandy's opinion, that men can bear misfortunes best in a recumbent position. I believe they sat where they originally collapsed to the end of the voyage.

When the confusion was at its height, some enterprising pilgrim spied the boats hanging on the davits ; instantly there was a rush over the skylights and gangways to obtain a seat in these coveted havens of refuge, and in less than five minutes there must have been twenty human beings in each boat. There they were, without awning or protection, with no room to *stir*, much less lie down, and there they proposed to remain for three or four days. Truly it is not

without reason that a Moslem calls himself ' one
of the resigned.'

The batch taken in at Suez were much poorer
and more travel-worn than those at Port Said ;
they had come from Tunis and Morocco, and
had doubtless suffered much. We had to pass
two nights in the Canal, owing to our bad luck
in getting behind a slow lazy collier, which lay
to for the night much earlier than she need
have done, thereby obliging us to lie to also.
We *hated* that collier, and when after leaving
Suez we saw a vessel on the rocks to the east,
we were all prepared to see in it an instance of
the eternal fitness of things had it been that
collier—but I believe it was not. The Captain
wished to go to the assistance of the unfortunate vessel, but the pilot was very unwilling to go any nearer the reefs with so large
a number of souls on board, and his advice
and that of the other ship's officers prevailed.
We consoled ourselves by thinking that the
sea was calm, and we saw Arab feluccas going
to the rescue ; but the Captain was sorely put

out and did not recover his spirits for some days.

Nov. 5.—Here we are, still in the Red Sea, but 200 miles south of Jeddah. The heat is very great and the cabins quite unbearable ; we sleep on deck under the stars, with only the Milky Way above us. How few people in England know what it is to sleep under the open sky. I do not altogether enjoy it—it makes me feel too small. We dine and breakfast on deck beneath a thick double awning, under which the heat is close on 100°.

We stopped at Jeddah only a day and a half, thanks to the energy of the Captain and crew in unlading cargo and pilgrims. The latter all came out in a striking metamorphosis the morning we anchored, for we had come in sight of the saddle-backed mountain overlooking Mecca, on seeing which every pilgrim must discard turban and shoes, and dress in nothing but Turkish towels. Some of the pilgrims were high Turkish officials from Constantinople, and they had sat every day on the quarter-deck, looking very dignified in their gold-embroidered uniforms, fez, and patent-leather shoes. To see them this morning come on deck with only a towel round their waists and another round their shoulders, leaving their fat arms bare, was a curious but not an imposing sight. They did not, however, appear the least shy, and were quite as stately and dignified as before, only the towels spoilt the effect. The English Consul had travelled with us from Suez, and at Jeddah very kindly invited us to go on shore and dine with him. He has a miniature steam launch which came out to meet him, and we went ashore in it. I never shall forget the intolerable heat of that steam launch ; we were sitting aft of the boiler and furnace, and not six feet from it, so that all its heat was blown back to us. The degree of heat was almost beyond human endurance, but in its intensity was almost comical. We simply gasped.

Jeddah is surrounded by coral reefs which prevent a vessel of any size approaching within a mile or more. A large English ship had

struck on a reef that morning, and was then
discharging her cargo in the hope of getting off,
which she did towards evening. On landing we
found the Consul's horses waiting, and a guard
of Egyptian soldiers. I was mounted on a fine
white Arab donkey, very large, and with enormous ears, and a bridle all hung with gay
tassels. The saddle was an Arab one, and my
seat on it sideways not of the firmest. A most
impetuous donkey he was, Selim by name, and
I was thankful to have an Arab groom holding
hard on to his head all the time. Selim occasionally lifted up his voice in a most powerful
and prolonged bray, when I trembled lest he
should wind up with a kick. However I
wronged this son of the desert; infidel though
I was he never threw me off.

The bazaar and most of the streets were
roofed in with frail-looking dilapidated board-
ing, which kept out the rays of the sun certainly, but kept in many evil smells. Most of
the good houses are built of coral; it is hewn
in great square blocks, and does not look as

romantic as it sounds. The streets are very narrow, and more or less blocked up by high wooden seats placed for the convenience of the shop-people and their customers. They were now also crowded with hundreds of camels and donkeys waiting for the transport of the pilgrims. We threaded our way miraculously through the sleeping dogs and kneeling camels, and the sweetmeat sellers and bales of goods, and I should have enjoyed the strangeness of the scene more had I not been so much occupied in keeping my seat on that pommelless saddle. Wriggling in and out as we did I could not assume quite the *dégagée* air I should have wished.

Arrived at the Consulate, a fine house profusely covered with wooden balconies, Venetian shutters, and woodwork of the most elaborate and picturesque kind, we were shown up certainly a hundred stone steps into a large upper room, overlooking the city and open to the four winds. It was furnished with wide divans, and divided by carved wooden arches and lattice-screens in Moorish style. Here we were offered coffee in Arab fashion ; it was quite black, and served in tiny little cups without handles. By each cup was standing a small egg-cup, but what use to put it to I did not know, till our host set the example of putting the coffee cup into the egg-cup ; you can then lift both together.

After resting till nearly sundown, we rode out with an escort to see Eve's tomb, which is outside the city wall. There can be no doubt she was a big woman, for there is her tomb to prove it ; it is nearly 400 feet long, with a little mosque in the centre, where the guide patted his stomach demonstratively to let us know which part of Mother Eve lay below. We then went to see the tanks and holes (called by courtesy wells) on which Jeddah depends for its water supply, and which in their turn depend on the rainfall. It only rains three or four times in the year, but then with such goodwill that all the tanks are filled enough to last some months.

Afterwards we rode through the Mecca gate, where only a few years ago they would have murdered a Christian for passing through ; and just outside we saw a caravan of some hundreds of camels preparing to start for Mecca. They have to go in great force for fear of the Bedouin Arabs. It was a strange sight ; the dreary hot expanse of yellow sand, unrelieved by a green blade or bush ; the white city wall and the white flat-roofed houses ; and a foreground of lean hungry dogs, camels kneeling and standing, loaded and unloaded, veiled women; some with little mats before their eyes, and rascally-looking picturesque Arabs in every style of dress and undress.

Jeddah is a very fanatical city, and only eleven years ago the people murdered every Christian there, consuls and all. A man-of-war was sent to shell the town, and hang as many ringleaders as could be caught, and there the matter ended.

We dined with the Consul, waited on by a Nubian who was captured in the Abyssinian War. Jeddah is a thriving slave market in spite of our having a gunboat cruising up and down the Red Sea for the suppression of the slave traffic ; but, as the Consul observes cheeringly, ' The market is no longer held *inside* the city walls,' so who shall say nothing has been done ? The boat in which Robert went ashore next day had a crew of four, out of whom three, they told him, were slaves. At ten o'clock we walked through the bazaar, deafened by the yelling of the dogs, who always are wakeful at night, to the shore, and the Consul sent us out to the ship in a four-oared boat ; the water was highly phosphorescent, and every time the oars dipped there was a swirl of light very pretty to see. So ended our day at Jeddah.

13

CHAPTER II.

ADEN — BOMBAY — ELEPHANTA — BURNING GHAUT — PARSEES' CRICKET — JOURNEY UP COUNTRY — AVERAGES UNSATISFACTORY.

Nov. 10.—We left Aden yesterday, and have now no halt before reaching Bombay, so we have fairly entered on Fytte ye Laste. The Captain expects to reach Bombay on Sunday, the 18th, which will bring our sojourn on board to exactly four weeks : it was a Sunday we sailed from Trieste, Sunday we reached Port Said, and Sunday we reached Jeddah. Now we shall have one Sunday in mid-sea, and the next should see us in harbour. We passed the Straits of Babel Mandeb during Wednesday night ; the difference of temperature was at once perceptible the moment we were out of that great stewpan the Red Sea ; the thermometer fell immediately to 86°, and the water in the bath felt absolutely cold.

Robert went ashore at Aden, but, having once been there and seen the barrenness of the land, I preferred staying on board and driving wonderful bargains with the evil-looking Jews who deal in ostrich feathers, and swarm up on the deck the moment a ship comes in. They shave their heads smooth, leaving only one long tuft on each side, which tuft they oil to a horrible extent and train into a long ringlet on either side of their face—the effect is ruffianly. They have the least conscience of any traders I ever met ; most men are content with asking twice or perhaps three times the value of the thing, but I cannot find that with these Jews the value bears any relation to the sum they ask ; a bundle of feathers for which they asked 8s. they ended by pressing on my acceptance for 1s. It was probably worth 6d.

The boys, too, who dive for sixpences always amuse me, with their shiny black bodies innocent of clothing, and their woolly wigs looking like close-fitting sponges ; they greatly exercised the quartermaster by clambering up on to the awning ; he grew very angry, and, taking a long pole in his hand, climbed up himself to drive them off. They enticed him into many difficulties by keeping only just beyond his reach, and, as soon as he had painfully crawled unpleasantly near, they one and all with a derisive shout leaped off into the sea.

In leaving Aden there was some excitement caused by the cable snapping which held us to the buoy and getting entangled with our screw ; the buoy was dragged right under the screw, and great fear was felt lest our precious screw should be injured ; fortunately no harm was done. We all still sleep on deck, and consequently have cool, pleasant nights ; the two Germans sleep under the dining-table, which makes a perfect four-poster and keeps off any dew. It is a trial when at dawn we have to go down to our cabins ; I lie down and try to sleep, but sleep is out of the question : the first grief is that a man comes round and shuts all the cabin windows, leaving us to breathe as best we can. He used to shut the dead-lights too, but

I made a stand against that, and threatened to complain to the Captain, so now only the window is shut, and that I can open for myself. This is preparatory to washing the deck. Then begins, within eighteen inches of your face as you lie in your berth, the most fearful stamping, banging, scraping, scrubbing, and squeaking (the latter caused I find by dragging an unwilling American chair across a wet deck). Yesterday they varied it by scrubbing the deck with pumice-stone. I could hear a load of it thrown down just above me, and felt very much as if my face were being scrubbed with it. All this time the water is sluicing down our window, so we dare not open it, and by the time the deck is clean we are nearly suffocated.

Then begin other noises, showing that the ship is awake. Sheep walk about and bleat; people begin drinking coffee and calling for the stewards. Yesterday the sailors set to work hammering out rivets from the iron mast, turning the ship into an iron foundry, and driving us all distracted. We remonstrated with the

Captain, who was somewhat annoyed, but has had the work stopped, so to-day we are enjoying the cessation of noise.

Bombay, Nov. 18.—I am not ungrateful for blessings, and am just now fresh from the enjoyment of one of the greatest earthly luxuries. To eat when hungry, to drink when thirsty, to get warm when cold—all these are delightful ; but I hardly think they come up to the supreme pleasure of feeling clean when you were not clean, and this is what I now feel for the first time for a month ! A bath on board ship is a delusive thing ; the water is salt and makes your skin feel sticky, the soap will not lather, and you are in such a state of heat all the time that you try to get it over as quickly as possible, and even then people come and rap at the door to try and hurry you out that they may come in. The luxury therefore of a very large tub in a cool room, with warm water, and plenty of time and space and soap, can hardly be understood by anyone who has never made the voyage to India in a steamer.

We anchored yesterday afternoon at five o'clock, and within a few minutes had transferred ourselves and our baggage to a native sailing-boat and were scudding away merrily to the shore; it took us nearly half an hour, for we had anchored far out, all the nearer places being already occupied. A large fleet, representing most of the countries in the world and including an enormous English troopship just arrived, was lying in the harbour, very picturesque in its variety.

We had been seized by an energetic Parsee tout, who even on board had marked us for his own, and had lured us by fair words and specious promises into going to his hotel. This was strongly opposed by another tout, who kept assuring us that 'first man, sir, speak nothing but lies,' a compliment the other returned with interest. Meanwhile we reached the landing-place, and vividly it brought to mind our first landing in India seven years ago. The same rows of carriages drawn up for their occupants to 'eat the air;' the same gorgeous Parsee turn-outs, some with a mounted bodyguard in attendance; Arab horses at every turn; the same silent-footed crowd; the same scent in the air. Had I been blindfold I should have known we had landed in India.

Our Parsee friend put us into, and the whole of our luggage on to, a one-horse rattle-trap, and away we drove, darkness falling rapidly, visibly, over the town; past the English quarter and its park and promenades, through the native city with its hot, narrow streets, till we at last pulled up at the Old Byculla Hotel, where we put up seven years ago. We have delightful rooms, opening on to a wide verandah which runs completely round the house; they are almost the same we had before, and the crows and the sparrows which hop familiarly about seem like old friends; I suppose I knew their great-grandfathers.

We told the hotel people I should want an ayah while we are here. This morning on waking an ayah appears, salaams, and brings a cup of tea in the most home-like manner;

she shows her testimonials from former mistresses, and I engage her. She falls into my ways immediately, as if she had been with me for years; unpacks, and arranges my room as if she had done so every day. Surely in no country but India can you get so much comfort for so small an outlay; she gets 12*l.* a year, and feeds herself.

Allahabad, Nov. 24.—Another stage of our journey is over, and a long and wearisome one of thirty-seven hours together in the train; the heat was not very trying, and at night went down to 62°, which is so much colder than anything we have had this side of the Canal that we were perished with cold, and were thankful to open our bundle of wraps and ulsters, things we have loathed the sight of till now. A friend of ours truly remarked that 'human nature unfortunately will not be satisfied with averages, and it is no consolation for being suffocated with heat all day, to lie awake with cold at night.'

First-class tickets give each person a

sleeping-berth, so that a long journey in India is far less fatiguing than one half as long in Europe. The carriages are large, and have cunningly devised beds which fold back out of the way in the daytime, and form a double tier of berths when let down.

Before leaving Bombay we made an expedition to the Caves of Elephanta; they look as if a race of giants must have hewn them, and stand grim and mysterious, defying both time and man. Men have done their worst on them; it is wonderful to think of the bitterness and persistency with which they carried out the work of (attempted) destruction; the rock is very hard, and enormous labour and time has been expended on destroying the colossal carved figures and pillars. The chief temple is a large low hall, having eight rows of huge carved pillars left in the natural rock; in many instances the destroyers have actually hewn away the whole of the pillar, and you see the great melon-shaped capital alone clinging to the roof.

In other places they have even succeeded in

hewing away the capital, and there it lies on the
ground like a gigantic melon weighing some
tons. On the walls are colossal figures from
the Hindu mythology ; all the lower part, as far
as men can reach, destroyed, but the upper part
is preserved. The faces have the same stern,
mournful look, as if they were gazing out into
eternity, such as there is on the Egyptian
Sphinxes ; there is something oppressive in such
sights. They seem to teach you so grimly and
silently that time is nothing, fame is nothing,
men are nothing.

The view from the plateau in front of them
is beautiful ; you ascend to the temples by
several hundred rock-hewn steps, their edges
fearfully sharp and clean-cut. The island is
covered with vegetation, chief among which is
the palm-tree, tamarind, and prickly-pear.
Looking back from the plateau you have a
grove of palms at your feet, and beyond that
the sea, studded with small islands and backed
by the Ghauts on the mainland, crowned with
their curious rocks looking like great fortresses.

Natives with very slight clothing on (a hand-kerchief makes quite a good suit) come and offer you old matchboxes, full of very beautiful and singular beetles, shining like burnished gold, and having a transparent circular plate round them, making them look like little tortoises.

We also went while at Bombay to see the Hindu Burning Ghaut. I cannot understand why so much fuss is made in Europe about cremation, and the various ways of accomplishing it, and of making it unobjectionable to the living, and the cost and so on, when the system in its simplest form may be seen every day in full work at Bombay, as it has been for thousands of years. Close to the most fashionable drive is the Burning Ghaut, where from twenty-five to fifty corpses are burnt daily, and through the gratings in the wall you can see the fires inside as you drive by of an evening. We went in and stood where we had a good view of the whole enclosure ; five fires were burning at the time, but the corpse on each had been already con-sumed. Our Hindu guide told us it takes three hours to consume the body, and the minimum cost is 6s. He pointed out one pile still burning, which he said was of sandalwood, and was the funeral pile of a very rich man ; the relatives were standing by pouring on rosin to keep up the flames, and when all was consumed they would gather up the ashes and throw them into the river. It is a method of disposing of the dead which seems to me to have many advantages.

The Parsees are a very progressive race ; among other English customs they have adopted is cricket, which they have taken up with great zeal. You may see the great plain covered of an evening with young Parsees playing in a promiscuous manner, the various sets of stumps so close together that I should think accidents must be frequent. Perhaps they do not bowl very fast ; certainly they wear no pads, and their shins are sharp.

Robert has just returned from reporting himself to the authorities, and brings the news that our destination is settled. We go to Meerut,

where he is to take up the post of Collector; it
is much the same as a Deputy Commissioner in
Oudh, save that the work is less and the pay
more.　Meerut is a very good station to be sent
to ; it is twenty hours by rail from here, and we
start to-morrow at midnight.

CHAPTER III.

MEERUT—A GARDEN IN A FORTNIGHT—ICE-MAKING—CHRIST-
MAS DAY—VEGETABLE TURKEYS—BALL AND BANDS.

Meerut, Nov. 27.—We have arrived at our
journey's end, and find this place cooler than
any we have yet reached ; the range indoors is
from 73° to 65°, which is very pleasant.   We are
stopping at a hotel, as our heavy baggage which
was to have met us at Bombay had not arrived,
and we have therefore absolutely nothing with
us beyond what luggage we had on the Con-
tinent, and are in great destitution.   Bags and
baggage are a nuisance—but the absence of them
is even a greater one.

Hotels in India are not hotbeds of luxury ;
last night, on desiring that our beds might be
made, we were told there were no sheets !
Hard wooden beds there were, with a thin and

ancient mattrass, through which the wooden frame showed like the ribs of an old cab-horse. We were told that 'those Sahibs who brought sheets had them,' which was cold comfort to us, who, not having brought them, had them not. Luckily we had a slight acquaintance with one gentleman in the station, and sent him a note begging for sheets and pillow-cases, with which he kindly supplied us, and, in spite of our bony beds, we slept the sleep of the tired. There are no mosquitoes here—it is too cold for them I suppose; at Allahabad they swarmed, and as I lay awake in the morning I could see forty or fifty of them looking through the curtains in a bloodthirsty way.

Of course the news spread like wildfire that the new Collector Sahib had arrived, and this morning the hotel was positively beleaguered with crowds of applicants for service. Two Government chuprassies (a kind of orderly) were luckily already in attendance on Robert, so they and our bearer, whom we engaged in Allahabad, kept off the crowd. Directly breakfast was over, Robert went to the Kutcherry to take over charge of his office, and I held a *levée* of servants; the only difficulty was to make a selection from so many candidates, but the bearer helped me, and within half an hour I engaged a cook, kitmagár, ayah and under-ayah, bhisti, sweeper, and washerman—so a beginning is made.

Now we have a house to find, and furniture, horses, carriages, cows, poultry—a fearful vista. We have also as new-comers to call on all the residents here, which means spending days in leaving cards on strangers, for this is a large civil and military station, with artillery, cavalry, and line regiments both British and native. Fortunately for us, we start one point above zero, for the 15th Hussars are here, and it will be a pleasure meeting the L——s again.

Robert's work will be a good deal lighter here than in Oudh, for work is distributed quite differently here in the North-West. All civil and all heavy criminal cases, both of which came before him in Oudh, are here tried by an independent judge, so the difference is immense. His district is a large one, having nearly 1,600 villages and a population of 1,300,000 souls; it is about fifty miles each way and very square, with Meerut in the centre; it is bordered on the east by the Ganges, and on the west by the Jumna, from Delhi northwards.

Nov. 29.—Still *in statu quo*—houseless and baggageless. The station is a pretty one, with quantities of trees about it, and a very fine Mall, said to be the finest in India. The roads are wide and smooth, of great extent, and (some of them) well watered, all of which we shall much appreciate in the hot weather. We have a longer and colder cold season here than in Oudh, and a much severer hot season, which seems unnecessary.

Yesterday I was delighted at getting a telegram from ' Peer Bux, Khansáma. Kindly telegraph if I come.' Peer Bux is our former head butler, the most useful servant we ever had. He is a man of some property at Fyzabad, and in good service there, so I am surprised at his volunteering to come to us here. We telegraphed, 'Come.'

Dec. 9.—At last we have succeeded in getting into a house of our own. We looked at several, and it would have amused you to have been with us and heard the anxious willingness of the men in charge to meet our wishes. One house had no garden of any kind ; it stood in the middle of a large rough field. We said we could not take a house that had no garden ; to which the man eagerly replied—'Certainly a garden was very necessary, and in fifteen days it should be quite ready.' I admire that man's power of rising to an emergency.

Having decided that this house would suit us, there remained the difficulty of getting into it without possessing any tables or things of our own. This was met by the landlord and another rich native, who at once said that in twenty-four hours they would furnish the house for us ; and in truth we came in two days later and found matting, carpets, furniture, crockery, lamps, cooking utensils, table linen, &c., all provided! We were very glad to leave the hotel, and have since been gradually collecting a few things of our own, which with our English furniture (which arrived from Calcutta yesterday) make us now nearly independent of borrowed goods.

All our china and glass we had packed up and left at Fyzabad two years ago, and the Khansáma brought it with him, as well as my dear old cat; we were so glad to see her again.

We like this house on the whole; the rooms are good, and all about twenty-four feet high, which gives us plenty of head room!—a want I often felt in England. There is a good garden, *not* made in fifteen days; but not much space for lawn-tennis courts.

Last night, to the joy of everyone except a few miserable people who have already gone into camp, the heavens were opened and we had a fall of three inches of rain. The natives are in great spirits; they say the great spring crop is now safe and likely to be a magnificent one. The immediate consequence of the rain is a fall of three to four lbs. per rupee in the price of grain and flour.

It was a tremendous storm, with a furious wind, and I should doubt any tents having withstood it ; we are sure to hear tales of grief in a day or two. Nothing indeed can be much more unpleasant than having a wet tent blown down atop of you, and if you happen to be in bed at the time so much the worse. That aggravation has been spared us, but we have known the sensation of being buried flat and hopelessly under a heavy drenching-wet tent. Had it not been for the non-arrival of our baggage we should now have been out in camp, so there is comfort to be found in that. I hope all our boxes are not at the bottom of the sea.

We have bought a carriage and a pair of Australian mares called here ' Walers,' and in advertisements sometimes ' Whalers ' by persons not great at derivations. They come with a very good character, but I always suspect new horses—there are so many things they *may* do.

Besides horses we have bought a cow, and

she is now grazing on the tennis-court, with a man sitting to watch her. Whether you have ten cows or one you must have a cowman—as if not how would she get milked ? So our man is not overworked, and has much time for profitable meditation.

Jan. 10, 1878.—The New Year has begun with great cold. If I tell you what the thermometer is you will be unable to sympathise with us, for it will not seem to you to be severe cold, but there is no doubt it is felt so here ; at night, out of doors, it has gone down to 31°, and in the day only goes up to 50°. This does not sound much in the way of cold I know, but people wear furs and ulsters and thickest winter clothing, and after all suffer from cold ; and the odd thing is that people just out from England feel the cold as much as others ! It has been a splendid year for filling the ice-houses, for you must know that though we do not get *skating* in India we get *ice*, and in this way. Acres of ground are covered with large shallow earthen saucers, and on a promising night these are

filled with water. About three o'clock in the
morning the cold is sufficient to freeze, for ice is
formed here at 34° I believe. Then about 2,000
coolies, poor shivering wretches, having been
collected, the whole of this ice is packed together, hurried off and stored in pits before
sunrise, and in this way they will make 50,000
or 60,000 lbs. of ice in one night. This is
the only way in which we can store up any
of our superfluous cold now to comfort us in
the days of superfluous heat we shall soon be
enduring.

Christmas came and went, as it generally
does in India, with nothing to make you feel it
to be more Christmas Day than Midsummer Day.
The church was elaborately decorated with
plantain-leaves, roses, poinsettias, violets, and
gorgeous creepers—some holly even had been
imported from the hills (*i.e.* the Himalayas) to
inspire seasonable feelings ; and as long as we
were in church the service and the hymns made
us feel it to be Christmas, but the impression
was over at the church door. The sight of the

troops in their pith helmets (for the sun is always powerful) and the total absence of any poor people are enough to destroy any resemblance to the Christmas of our youth.

We tried to get up a treat for poor children, and collected about forty who were certainly poor, but chiefly half-castes, and not having much resemblance to English village children. However, they stuffed themselves with cake and buns and oranges in thoroughly orthodox fashion, and possibly felt that it was Christmas.

The principal feature of the day is the swarms of natives who come to make their salaam to Robert, beginning early in the morning and going on till noon. They all bring offerings too, which it is a disgrace to them to have refused; and the hall is piled with trays of sweetmeats, fruit, toys, and anything they venture to offer. It is forbidden to offer anything but fruit and vegetables, but the devices they resort to in order to evade this are very amusing; among other things two turkeys were marched

in as one man's offering. Robert looked dis-
pleased, and said he could not accept such
things, whereupon the man pleaded earnestly
that they were *vegetable* turkeys ! It was impossible to resist this ; Robert merely told him
that in future even vegetable turkeys could not
be allowed. At present these singular birds are
stalking about the grounds, gobbling wonderfully
like common turkeys.

There has been a ball given by the Hussars,
and private theatricals, and endless dinner
parties, not to mention tennis and Badminton
parties. To-night there is a ball given by us
civilians and the staff to the regiments. Robert
is on the committee, and his department is the
lighting, decorating, and furnishing. There has
been quite a storm in a teacup about the music ;
two regimental bands were asked to play, and
the man entrusted with the music department
arranged that one band should play up to supper-
time, and the other afterwards. Unfortunately
the proverb relating to the event of two men
riding on one horse seems never to have reached

Meerut, and bitter was the feeling in the regiment whose band was told off to play after supper. It is strange how difficult it is to arrange any matter without hurting somebody's feelings.

CHAPTER IV.

IN CAMP—BEATING IN KNOWLEDGE—TIGER TELEGRAM—BABY
CAMEL—DELHI—UNPOPULARITY OF LORD LYTTON—GLOBE-
TROTTERS—KHANSAMA AND EGGS.

Jan. 23, 1878.—Once more we find ourselves in camp, but in a sadly diminished one
compared with our former ones, when the
children's tent and the children's carriage and
horses and ponies and ayahs formed the principal
part of it. Now we have only a single pole-
tent and a large flat-topped square tent called a
Shamiana, in which Robert does his work and
we breakfast and dine. This humble camp is
now all we require. The kitchen servants have
a small tent to sleep in, but the rest sleep where
they can, and very cold they must find it; but
no one dreams of complaining, as it is part of
the natural order of things.

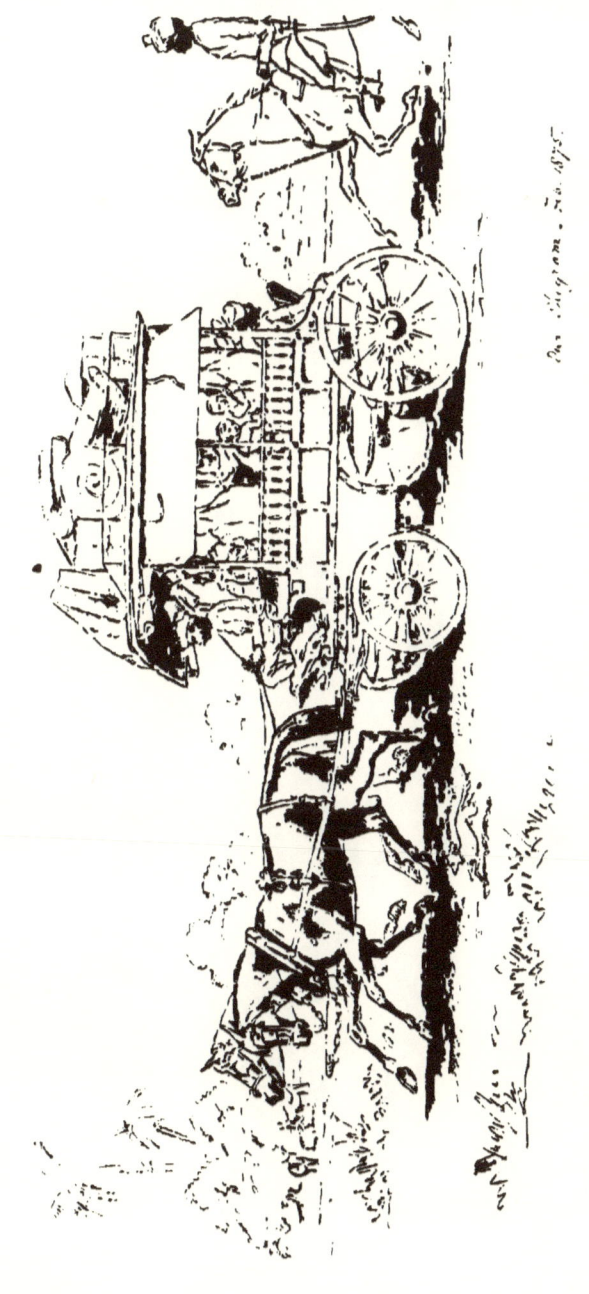

Even the cow has to wear a blanket, and being an unsophisticated cow she resents it, kicks off the blanket, and kicks furiously at the cowman for putting it on again ; but she will soon learn that a blanket is a good thing, though artificial. She has not yet taken kindly to camp life, the constant marching disturbs her, and she is so inconsiderate as not to give any milk on coming in from a march. But this, too, will all come right when she is better educated.

Our tents and everything are carried on camels ; they are more troublesome than carts to load, but once laden they stride away without minding whether the road be good or bad, and never stick fast in a rut or roll down a bank as carts are apt to do on a dark night. We have them kept a long way from our tents, both on account of the horrible noises they make and of their smell, which is powerful exceedingly, and is one of the odours of Araby I prefer being to windward of. We have no elephants with us now, as their keep is expensive and the sport here not worth it—at any rate not till we march near the Ganges.

Robert has two camel orderlies with him, one of whom always escorts our carriage on the march, and with perfect ease keeps up with us at a shuffle of eight or nine miles an hour. A camel goes along on his spongy feet as silently as a cat, and has to wear a collar of bells to warn people of his approach. Sometimes the orderly ties up or muffles the bells, and I have a feeling that the camel may suddenly stretch forward and bite my shoulder before I am aware he is near. However, his head is always reined up very high by the driving cord passing through his nose.

' Cord ' reminds me of my Macramé lace ; did I tell you how much the Turkish ladies on board ship admired it, and how my old ayah is so taken with it that I have promised to teach her how to make it ? She herself has great faith in the power of *beating* knowledge in. She told me how years ago she had been taught the clock, and soon learnt the hours, but the minutes she could never understand till one day

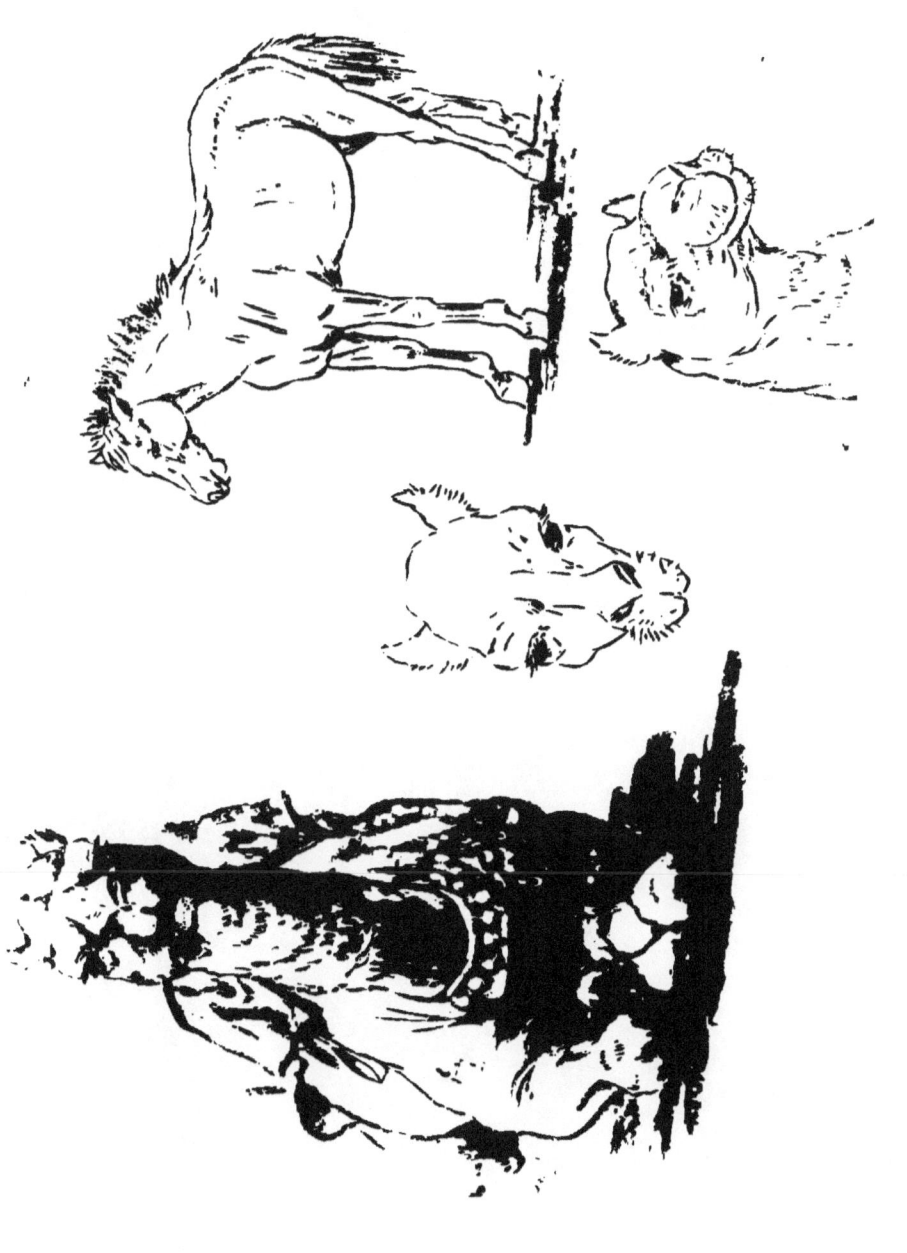

the 'Mêm Sahib' who was teaching her grew angry, and smote her, *not* so lightly, on the cheek. From that day, she assures me, her memory improved—the minutes no longer were a mystery. The same lady taught her to knit and sew, most rare accomplishments in a native woman, and she seems to have received divers sound cuffs to help her memory in those also. She cheerfully allows their efficacy. She is an intelligent old woman, of a very different type to a bright genius I once had, who with misplaced patience tried perseveringly to button my boots *with a corkscrew*! She knew it was done with some foreign instrument, and her intelligence had not grasped the principle of a button-hook.

The great Mahommedan Festival of the Moharram came last week, and rumours were rife in Meerut that a rising was impending. Robert was away in camp, and though I knew he did not attach any weight to the report, yet I own I was heartily glad when the day of the expected outbreak was fairly over. There is no doubt we live on a volcano in India, with the elements of an eruption always seething below the surface. In this instance the apprehension does not appear to have been confined to Meerut, as an officer wrote from Lahore to say that there it had been felt more strongly, and that, though all outward show had carefully been suppressed, the troops had all been under orders how to act if occasion arose. In Meerut the rumours were traced to the station-master, whose servants told him they had travelled in the train with two Mussulmans, who had said that on the day of the Moharram all the infidels were to be massacred. The station-master was out of his mind with fright, and telegraphed to headquarters to be immediately transferred.

This reminds me of an amusing telegram sent by a station-master in the Central Provinces to his official superior : ' Tiger jumping in station yard. Pointsman unable to go to points through fear. Please arrange sharp.'

Jan. 26.—A rainy day in camp. Not a hopeless one, but one that keeps us full of anxiety as to what may come. We sat at breakfast in the great Shamiana, which is eminently a fair-weather

tent, and in rain has to be half-struck, when it
assumes a forlorn and wretched appearance, with
its gay fringe and lappets draggling in the wet,
looking as melancholy as a bed of poppies after
a thunderstorm. It is also very unpleasant
then to sit in, for besides being wet and open to
the winds (as the side walls have to be removed
when in this position), it has a tendency to
collapse altogether should a gust of wind get
under it, all of which tends to make you eat
your breakfast without dawdling, and, as it were,
with your loins girded for flight.

We have found shelter for most of the
animals, but I am disturbed about a baby camel
only two days old ; it would be easy to shelter
him in a tent, but his mother is a difficulty
which may be described as enormous. If she
came in no one else could, and the baby would
not come without her. So I can only hope his
soft grey woolly coat will keep him from suffering from the wet. He was born two nights ago,
and the very next morning the camel-driver
made him set off on a ten-mile march to the

next camp on his own weak shaky legs; he had no idea, poor baby, how to use them, they were constantly and unexpectedly shutting up like a two-foot rule, and he lay down so often in the first half-mile that at last the camel-driver tied him up in a blanket and slung him on his mother's back. How very rough he must have found it! If it were not for his coat we should see he was black and blue. He is the most quaint uncouth baby I ever saw; his neck is like a swan's, and he has a small, short, woolly body supported on four enormous, big-jointed, badly-made legs, very shaky and unmanageable, always spreading out in some unwished-for direction.

Feb. 1.—Yesterday we moved our camp to Shádera, and found our tents pitched within sight of the mosques and minarets of Delhi. Our Mahommedan servants are delighted, as they will all beg leave to go into the city. In the afternoon Robert and I drove in, getting there rather late, as we had to wait nearly half an hour before being able to cross the great Jumna bridge. It is an iron bridge about half

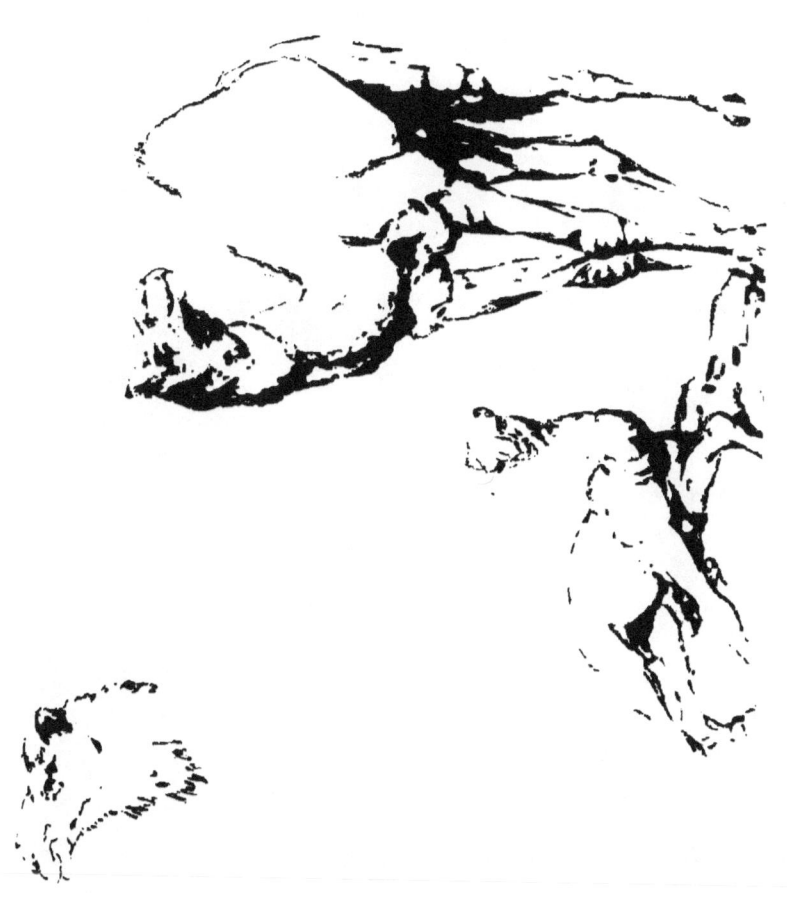

a mile long, with a covered way for carriages and foot-passengers, while the trains run overhead; our horses would have gone mad with fright if a train had crossed while we were on the bridge, but we took very good care to ascertain that no train was due. The cartway is so narrow that nothing can pass anything, so if even a laden bullock is on the bridge at the far end you have to wait until he emerges at your end. The man in charge at each end puts up a signal to stop any further admissions when there are carts at his end ready to cross, but still they have to wait until the long file already on the bridge has crawled out. It is a horrible bridge, and instead of paying two rupees, as we did, for the pleasure of crossing, we would gladly have paid twice that to avoid the bridge altogether, but there was no alternative short of giving up Delhi.

We drove along under the great red stone walls of the old Mogul's Palace, the scene of such desperate fighting in '57, and I could not help feeling that those walls are surely destined to see other struggles as fierce and bloody.

Delhi is apparently marked out by nature and fate to be the battle-field of India. I should like to have been there at the Proclamation of the Queen as Empress ; it must have been a splendid pageant, and as an historical event is not likely to be equalled by anything in our lifetime. It is a pity it should have been so managed as to cause such deep dissatisfaction among the whole body of English in India, for, though it is well to treat the natives with courtesy and consideration, it is ill to treat the English with conspicuous want of both. The natives are shrewd, and quite alive to the contrast ; one of them said to an English officer who was complaining of some slight, ' You should stain your face brown, and then you would get anything you want.'

The feeling of dissatisfaction throughout the army was strong and universal. I have heard men of all branches of the service speak of it, English and native cavalry, artillery, line ; but there is only one feeling amongst them—that of deep-felt disgust at the way they were treated. It seems that the whole of the troops, a magnifi-

cent force such as has never before been assembled
in time of peace, were posted two miles from the
scene of the Proclamation, and kept under arms
under a burning sun for three hours, out of sight
and out of hearing ; and when it was represented
to the Viceroy that much discontent was felt, and
that it would gratify the troops if they were
allowed to march past at the close of the proceedings, permission was refused.

It is said that a good deal of mischief is
being done by the fashionable visitors who now
flock to India in the cold season, are delighted
and flattered by all the novelty of native hospi-
tality, courtesy, and often servility, and to whom
the English officials are of course in no way
either novel or interesting, and who then return
home and spread the idea that the English in
India require snubbing and the trusty natives
exalting. It may be so, but these passing visitors
are not in a position to be good judges. A visi-
tor can only see things very superficially, he is
wholly irresponsible, and he finds it pleasant to
pose as a kind of champion, and be lavishly gra-

cious to the natives and studiously cold to his fellow-countrymen. If his life were cast, as theirs is, among these same natives, he would find this enthusiasm and novelty wear off. He would find that a gulf was fixed between him and men who, however long their acquaintance, would never admit him into their home life, would consider their wives and daughters insulted if he so much as alluded to them, would sooner die than eat at his table, and who in their inmost heart would not sorrow if every Christian were driven into the sea.

While Robert was having a Turkish bath at Delhi, I drove about the bazaar and chose some brasswork and a few other specimens of native work, but at the bearer's earnest request I only *selected* certain things, and have to-day sent him in to make his own bargains for them. He is a wonderful man at a bargain, and it distresses him to see me offer more for a thing than he considers it worth. I am really quite ashamed sometimes to confess to him what I have given for a thing, and as he keeps all the money I can never get off without confession. I doubt his driving a bargain to-day with the brass-worker ; the man professes to ask *prix fixe*, but the bearer scouts the idea, and feels his credit involved in getting the things for less than the man asked me.

Once, in Meerut, I wanted some calico, and Mrs. D—— told me it ought only to cost twelve rupees the piece. Armed with this information, I sent for a cloth merchant, who showed me the quality required, but swore with many oaths that its price was thirteen and a half, and no-where could it be bought for less. I assured him it had been bought for twelve. Nothing would shake him, and as neither of us would give in, the bargain fell through, and he gathered up his bundles and departed. The bearer was present, and even he was shaken as to the value of the calico. However, he took his stand on this, that *if* Mrs. D—— had bought it for twelve rupees it was ridiculous to suppose that he, Chaudri Rám, should not be able to get it for less. So out he sallied, and finally brought me in triumph the identical quality, for which he had paid eleven and a half. Robert's opinion is that, rather than allow that he could not beat Mrs. D—— at a bargain, he would have paid the half-rupee out of his own pocket!

He is somewhat distressed at the charges made by the Khansáma, who certainly does write down a surprising amount of eggs and other things supposed to be consumed by Robert and me, but, being an excellent servant in other ways, I rather wink at his accounts. Sometimes I own I have to wink hard, and cannot always refrain from a smile; but if ever I venture mildly to say that the number of eggs is really astonishing, I have them all, so to speak, thrown at my head, and have to listen to a voluble account of how many went to the soup, and the rissoles, and the salad, and the pudding, and the anchovy toast, till I am quite suppressed, and ready to declare that we could not possibly have dined with an egg less. Being, however, a woman, and convinced against my will, it is not surprising that I should be of the same opinion still.

CHAPTER V.

EASTERN JUMNA CANAL—DIFFERENCE OF OPINION ABOUT CANALS—JÂTS AND HIGH FARMING—ENGINEERS AND THEIR BRIDGES—HAWK AND HARE—DIFFICULTIES OF MARCH.

Feb. 4.—For the last three days we have been marching and camping on the banks of the Eastern Jumna Canal. It is quite a new experience to me, and the drives prettier than any we have seen before in India. As yet the Canal is quite small, for we are at its outlet end, and it had never struck me before that an irrigation canal is exactly the reverse of a river in that respect ; for it begins very large and broad, and gradually narrows, until at its outlet (having been drained all along its course by branch irrigation cuts) it is reduced to a six-foot wide ditch.

This is an old canal, and has a beautiful belt

E 2

of trees along both banks, originally planted, but since left to nature, and now looking quite wild, with an undergrowth in many places of impenetrable thorns, creepers, and bamboos. Numbers of monkeys live along here and cause great damage to the crops. You see them sit-ting by scores in the fields, helping themselves to the grain with a liberality and an air of owner-ship that must be highly vexing to a taxpayer. They look upon us as intruders, and make hideous threatening faces at us as we go by. One of them met with a delightful punishment just now ; we were sitting in our tent, when we heard a heavy fall into the water. On running out to see who had fallen in, we found it was an old monkey, who, in attempting to jump from a tree on this side to one on the opposite bank, had missed the branch and fallen with this tremendous splash into the Canal. I hope his cold bath will make him humbler.

We have told our men to drive the monkeys out of this grove with golails (bows which throw stones), which is the only weapon really

dreaded by them. They do not much mind a
gun, knowing very well it is an empty threat.
and that you will not shoot them. But they
know you will hit them with a stone if you can,
so a general scamper takes place when a golail
is produced.

The trees swarm with parrakeets, chattering
and swinging and swooping about in the gayest
spirits, their lovely green plumage glistening
brilliantly as they dart through the grove in
flocks.

Feb. 6.—To-day we left the Canal banks, for
which I am quite sorry. When one sees the
pleasant broad stream flowing along through the
dry plain, and sees the belt of fine trees all along
it, and the numberless little aqueducts leading
off it to water the fields, it seems as if canals
. must be undoubted blessings. And yet, if there
be one thing more than another on which
opinion in India is divided, it is as to the merits
of canal irrigation. It is not that one party
considers it of greater benefit than the other
does ; it is not a difference of degree but of kind.

One party considers the welfare of India to depend on canal irrigation. The other considers canal irrigation to be absolutely pernicious to the land. I have positively *no* opinion in the matter ; the two views seem too perplexing and irreconcilable for an outsider to be able to form an opinion. Each side hurls hard facts at the other to prove the impossibility of holding any view but one. Is it not strange that in a question of such immense importance—and which you would think could be settled once and for ever by a careful survey of results—it should still be possible for two parties of men, each possessing equal knowledge and experience of the subject, to hold diametrically opposite opinions ? What is truth indeed ? .

An English landowner in this district who has a large estate, which he has farmed and managed successfully for the past fifteen years, was talking over this canal question with Robert, and gave it as his opinion distinctly that canals were most pernicious, and in this district alone cause a loss amounting to many thousand pounds annually. He has undoubtedly much experience, and this opinion is the result of it. Is it not then perplexing to hear men of equal experience urge the very contrary view? If opinions in a practical matter like this cannot be reconciled by facts and demonstration, what indeed is the use of disputing—much less of breaking heads—about abstract questions whose very nature does not admit of demonstrative proof?

Feb. 10.—The last two days I have been out on an elephant for a stroll with Robert, who took his gun, and we beat some sugar-cane, but with no result beyond bagging five jackals. Their skins make a very good rug, and their flesh too is not wasted, for, strange to say, there is a certain caste, something like gipsies, who eat snakes, rats, and even jackals; so they gladly skin them for us in return for being allowed to take the carcase.

We saw numbers of pea-fowl, but never shoot any for mere sport, only when the pot is empty. We had them driven, as it is such a pretty sight to see them rise in a flock, and easily top the highest trees. Their gorgeous array, whatever the price of grain may be, is a great contrast to the miserable rags generally worn by the villagers on whose crops they live. No one thinks of killing them, hardly even of driving them away ; the belief is that feeding God's wild creatures brings a blessing on the crops—so the pigs and the pea-fowl and parrots, and the monkeys and the antelope, are allowed to roam about and feed where they like. How different from the spirit of English farmers!

Along the line of march yesterday and to-day we have noticed how much finer the crops were than in other parts of the district. Robert says they belong to a caste called Jâts, who are free from most Hindu caste prejudices, and make excellent agriculturists accordingly, being able to use good manures and to plough with-out loss of caste. Besides this they are very hard-working, and you can see at once that they are a more thriving people—better fed and better clothed than the generality of villagers. They

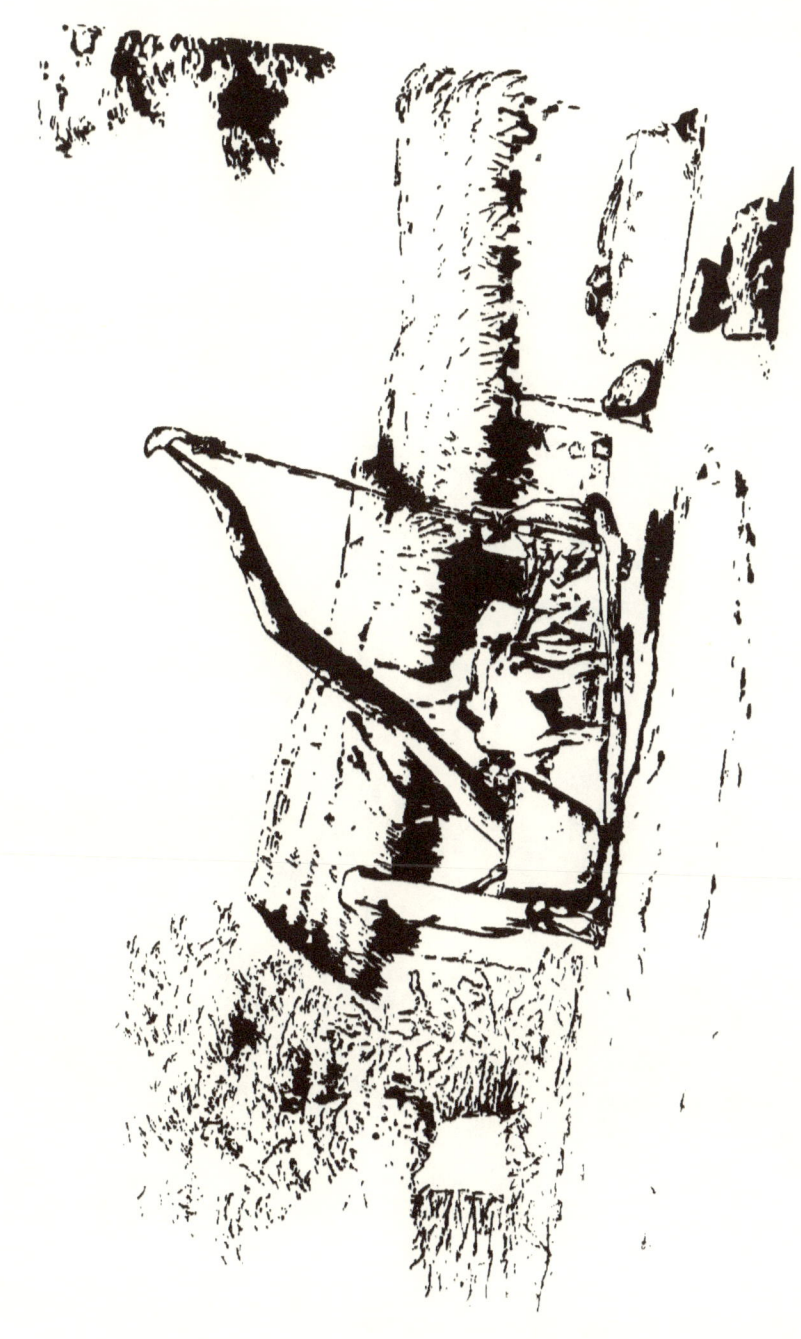

form the principal population in this neighbourhood, and the crops everywhere bear witness to
their high farming.

We are encamped close to the little town of
Baraut, which is said to be 1,100 years old.
I dare say it looks now very much as it did in
days when England was chiefly fen and forest.
Our marches are all on level ground, as this
great Gangetic plain we are on is an absolute
flat, formed of deep alluvial soil. It is a country
that has more dogs and less stones to throw at
them than any other. The only slope the
carriage ever goes up or down is when crossing
the various bridges over canals and streams,
which bridges the engineers for inscrutable
reasons, not to be understood by common
minds, invariably build after the pattern of a
camel's back ; this necessitates an embankment
for some distance on either side, which embankment, being cut away more or less by every
heavy rainfall, has to be constantly repaired.
It also gives everyone a chance of rolling down
its sides should a horse shy. Beyond this no

ordinary mind can conceive the reason for raising the bridges so much above the road level, but it is a cherished practice of Indian engineers.

Another happy practice is to dig huge ditches, from three to eight feet deep, and with straight sides perfectly unfenced, along the sides of almost all roads, but more especially in stations where the traffic is constant. The engineers call them drains; the unreasoning public call them man-traps and other hard names, and have committees to protest against them. But in vain; the ditches grow deeper—and at length the gloomy conviction is being forced on us that nothing short of the death of the Lieutenant-Governor, or possibly the Chief Engineer, by breaking his neck in one, will cause any steps to be taken to protect the public.

Feb. 11.—When out shooting yesterday we saw an unusual incident. A hare had been put up by the beaters, but out of shot; we were watching her scudding away, when suddenly a large hawk swooped down on her, and a piteous cry told us that he had struck her. Robert ran up to the spot and drove off the hawk, who dropped the hare, but it was stone dead. We never before saw a hawk strike such large game. Native gentlemen often keep hawks for sporting purposes, but those we have seen used only to kill partridges.

Feb. 12.—A heavy thunderstorm yesterday, with torrents of rain. Luckily all preparations had been made for it ; the animals sent into the village for shelter, and an extra tent pitched to put the carriages and other things under. Ridges of earth had also been banked up all round the tents, owing to which we escaped being utterly flooded, as within ten minutes of the storm breaking we had a rapid muddy stream many inches deep flowing on all sides of us. Men were immediately at work cutting drains in all directions to carry off the water, and very shortly I counted twenty-three people, cutting and carrying earth, draining, and banking, with true native goodwill and energy in an emergency. Of course our tents are soaked, and necessitate an extra day's halt to dry them,

but at least the ground under us is dry, and
that is the main point.   We are vexed at having
to halt, as we are anxious to be at Meerut by
the 16th, when Roberts, the Billiard Champion,
is to play at the Club, and now it will involve
hard marching to get there in time.   Ladies are
to be admitted to see him play—a point obsti-
nately opposed by some of the members ; I think
it was finally carried by Mr. M——'s giving a
very happy turn to the matter.   He said that for
his part he thought the members were really *a
very respectable body of men,* and that there was
nothing to make the presence of ladies undesir-
able !   This was such a delightfully new point
of view that the opposition members suffered
themselves to be overpowered by their own
respectability !

The only other excitement in store for
Meerut is the running for the Pigsticker's Silver
Cup in March, when very good riding is sure to
be seen.   The boars are found on the low land
along the Ganges, much of which is very nasty
riding ground, full of hard tussocks of grass

and hidden holes. The competitors divide into several parties, and those in each party who get a 'first spear' (*i.e.* into the boar) have then to find a fresh boar and compete among themselves for the Cup. You can fancy what bold and reckless riding there is under such excitement. If the heat be not too great we shall be out in tents to see the meeting.

Feb. 13.—Yesterday's sun and wind having fairly dried the tents, we marched this morning. The road was in a dreadful state, and my carriage only able to go about four miles an hour; to-morrow's march is reported to be worse, so we shall have bullocks to draw the carriage.

The wet slushy state of the roads is very bad too for the camels, who, laden as they are, slip terribly. My foolish old cat wandered away from the camp last night, and had not returned when we marched this morning; if she be not eaten by jackals we shall recover her, as hunger will drive her to some village, and the news has gone forth far and wide that a 'Government cat' is lost !

Feb. 16.—Our march on the 14th was a very hard one, as we had feared. We ourselves performed it on the elephant, and so had no trouble, as it is a matter of perfect indifference to an elephant whether the ground be swampy or rough, whether the fords be deep or the bridges rotten—in the latter case he avoids them, and wades through the river. And he can go in safety up or down the most precipitous banks, where nothing but a goat would venture, for he takes each step with great caution, and acts on the maxim 'Never put out your foot farther than you can draw it back again.' When the bank is very steep he first kneels down, so that at any rate he cannot fall; he then cautiously slides down on his hind knees, and with both fore-legs stretched out stiffly; the angle is not a pleasant one for his riders, but you soon learn to hold on, and you are perfectly sure that if *you* do not fall the elephant will not.

The kitchen-cart and one other, as well as the camels carrying the advance-tents, go on over-night—as soon as they can pack up after

Varlets ...
Ye saïlode oie. K.

Ye Tarn sboïlce

our dinner—and that night they had a terrible march. In crossing one wretched ill-made bridge of boats one of the bullocks got both his fore-legs through the bridge, and it took much time and trouble to get him out without breaking his legs. The carts did not reach the new camping-ground till after daybreak.

When we arrive at nine or ten o'clock and find our tents pitched, the chairs and couches placed as we like them, and the table ready laid for breakfast, we can little realise the trouble and fatigue the servants have gone through since we last sat down to table the evening before, ten miles back.

CHAPTER VI.

WE are now in camp at Sardhana, a curiously
interesting place, twelve miles from Meerut, and
with a strange history.   Rather more than one
hundred years ago there was a certain Walter
Reinhard, described as a soldier of fortune, who
I imagine fought for any one who could pay him
well, and no doubt amassed much wealth in a
sufficiently discreditable way.   In 1777 he was
given large estates in this district, belonging
then to the Mahrattas—from whom we conquered
it in 1803— and lived here as a small prince with
a little army of his own.   Here he died in 1781,
leaving all his immense estates to his wife, a
native lady, known as the Begum Sumru (a

name Reinhard had adopted). She lived on here, keeping up her army—officered entirely by Europeans—and managing her estates with much energy and ability.

Soon after her husband's death she became a Christian, and proceeded to build a fine Roman Catholic church here, which she endowed liberally, and to establish a college of priests, also with a fine endowment; which church and college are still flourishing. A great number of her tenantry naturally adopted her new religion, the more so as loaves and fishes followed conversion, in the shape of the enjoyment of the interest on 5,000*l.* settled on them by the Begum. To this day, therefore, there is a little colony of Roman Catholics here; they do not increase in number, as their religion is now purely hereditary.

The Begum also built a fine palace here; there are many paintings in it—notably of the Begum herself, always represented in coloured silk trousers, with a full, perfectly transparent, muslin skirt reaching to her knees. She had no children, and Reinhard had only a natural son

who died, leaving a daughter. This daughter the
Begum took in hand, and presently married to
Mr. Dyce, an officer in her service. They had
a son, commonly known as Dyce Sombre, an
English corruption probably of Sumru ; and
here comes the strangest part of the story—this
Dyce Sombre married in 1840 a daughter of
Lord St. Vincent.

Sombre died at Paris many years ago—his
body being brought here and buried in the
church—and his widow married Lord Forrester,
and is now the owner of this property and
palace. She is called the Begum, the old
historical Begum having died in 1836.

It is a most curious history, and there is a
good deal I do not understand about it. The
main part of the old Begum's possessions lapsed
at her death to the British Government—why,
I do not know—so Lady Forrester has only a
small estate here, and had a long lawsuit before
getting even that.

Feb. 20.—We went to see Mr. Roberts play
on Monday, but he was not playing well, and

had only got up to 750 when his opponent won
the game. Roberts had given him 600 ; and as
the two were playing that night it was more
than he could do. His largest break was
64, made chiefly by the most delicate cannon
play, very pretty and wonderful to watch.
After the game was over he showed us some
tricks with the balls, which were simply a kind
of sleight-of-hand, but wonderful as showing his
command over the balls. He took the three balls
in his hand, and, standing at the 'spot' end of
the table, he said, 'In the baulk circle,' and
proceeded to throw each ball with great force
into the circle, where it suddenly stopped as if
seized by an invisible hand; the effect was
miraculous.

The Club paid him 600 rupees for two nights'
play—at which rate he must make a large income.
A French Billiard Champion is now in India, but
he and Roberts would not play a match, as each
is so superior at his own game. They say the
Frenchman could give Roberts 500 in 1,000 on
a French table.

Feb. 22.—Still in Meerut, but we go into camp again to-morrow. Our few days have been quite gay after our month of camp life, during which we only saw a white face three times. On Wednesday there were theatricals and tableaux vivants at the Melvilles'—the tableaux done extremely well. The first was to my mind too sad a subject for representation—it was from the picture 'Home they brought her warrior dead,' and there were three scenes to illustrate the verses which were sung by unseen singers.

During the intervals we were enlivened by singing which it was a real pleasure to listen to; the singers were Mrs. Le M——and her daughter. Mrs. Le M—— is a Greek, and sings as no Englishwoman ever does. She married at fifteen, and looks like an elder sister of her daughter.

Lord Dalkeith has been here this week on a visit to General Hardinge; he is away on what he calls 'sick leave,' and says he is not likely to visit India again, as he must not try his constituents too far.

We have lost our old Khansáma Peer Bux! He found that he could not play first fiddle so long as our present bearer is with us, and he would not fall so low as to play second. His market too was spoiled by the bearer's vexatious honesty, and by his annoying habit of informing me of the cheapest places to buy poultry and so on.

We saw his discontent brewing in camp, and were quite prepared on returning here to learn, as we did, that his grandmother was dead, and that he must go home *on a month's leave.* This fiction he kept up to the end; but as we happened to know of many preparations for departure he had made, such as selling his pony and sending off his servant to Fyzabad (for, if you please, this great man had a servant), we were not in any way deceived, and made our arrangements accordingly, knowing well that we shall see his face no more. I shall miss him, no doubt, but really his 'eggs' had assumed such proportions that I could not have winked much longer.

We have been having the punkahs out from

their winter retreat, and overhauling them for
necessary repairs and decoration, so that they
may be ready to hang on our return from camp.
They are made differently here to what they are
in Oudh; there the punkah-bar is simply a
heavy polished pole, with a deep heavy flounce
of calico hanging from it. Here it is a kind of
flat frame, sixteen inches wide, from which the
flounce hangs. This frame is generally merely
whitewashed, and very ugly, but is of course
capable of decoration. I am having ours painted
with a simple border taken from a fifteenth-cen-
tury missal, in two colours only, and it looks
very well.

Each punkah-frill takes fifteen to eighteen
yards of calico, besides some Turkey red or
other bordering to edge the flounces; so they
are quite expensive necessaries, costing about
13s. each, not counting the flat frame, which is
provided by the landlord. We shall have to
hang ten at least.

Imagine my feelings on returning from camp
to find that our zealous landlord had retinted

the drawing-room walls a bright pea green, my carpet borders being pale blue ! I thought the matter over for three days, but have finally told him he must absolutely do the walls over again, as it would be too painful to live in the house as it is. He can at least afford it, being a very rich native, rich enough and loyal enough to have just lent the Government 100,000*l*. without interest.

Mowána, Feb. 27.—In camp again. The roads worse than ever—unmetalled and nothing but rows of deep ruts. It is impossible to drive a pair, so we put in one horse and go about five miles an hour ; we were obliged to get five or six coolies to push in several places where there were deep sand-drifts over the road. As long as we are on these roads we shall make our marches on an elephant, as it is quite as quick and not so wearisome as the carriage.

There is no sport just about here ; we see antelopes, but Robert does not care about stalking them. There are plenty of wolves about, but they rarely give anyone a chance of getting

a shot at one. Only last year a wolf came
into the village here by daylight and carried off
a boy six years old, and got clear off with him,
and nothing more was ever seen of the poor
child. Another child was saved by its mother
catching hold of the wolf's hind-legs, and
pluckily holding him until the neighbours came
running up to help, when the brute dropped the
child.

We heard yesterday of my foolish old cat
having come to an Englishman's house close to
the camp where she ran away. It is ten days
since we lost her, and as she arrived with a
piece of string round her neck it is evident she
had been tied up in some native house. She
hates the natives, so no doubt took the first
opportunity to escape. We have sent a coolie
to fetch her, who will have a tramp of thirty
miles there and perhaps fifty back, as we shall
have moved further on by the time he returns.

March 1.—We are now encamped on the
low land by the Ganges, and had a visit last
night from a tiger, which came prowling and

roaring about our camp, frightening the elephant
so that he broke loose and escaped. We slept
too sound to be waked, but as the sentries and
watchmen, of whom there are twelve, all say
they heard the tiger there is no doubt one came,
and the villagers say there are several in a reedy
swamp a few hundred yards distant. Unfortunately the swamp abounds with quicksands, so
neither men nor elephants can venture in, and
there is no means of getting at the tigers that
may be there.

I should like to hear a wild tiger roar, but
am such a hopelessly sound sleeper that the
chances are against it.

March 2.—I have heard him! Last night
he came again, and roared tremendously. My
ayah, who had ventured outside the tent, came
running back in a fine fright, but he did not
come very near.

Yesterday I went out with Robert shooting,
each of us on an elephant, and we passed swamps
where fifty tigers might safely harbour ; all we
saw was the footprints of a tiger, quite fresh,

with the water oozing into the deep prints. The brute had evidently slunk away on hearing shots, and as Robert was then on foot and the ground rough and swampy I was thankful we did *not* see more than the footprints.

Our larder is just now well supplied, and I have had a game pie made, composed of partridge, sandgrouse, hare, antelope, peacock, and wildfowl. I hope it will be a success.

The climate here is decidedly cooler than at this time in Oudh. I am still wearing a cashmere gown, and we still find the stove pleasant in the evening. At night we have three or more blankets. The sun of course is hot, but not more as yet than you can bear with a lined umbrella.

March 5.—Yesterday we made a shooting march to this place, Ferózpúr, and as we knew it would take several hours we were up at half-past five, and off on our elephants at a quarter-past six, just as the edge of the sun was visible on the horizon through a grove of cocoa-nut palms. The grass was white with a thick dew, and the air fresh and delicious. I thoroughly agree with those who say that sunrise is the most delightful time of the twenty-four hours in India —indeed there can be no doubt about it. At the same time I hold that any pleasure may be bought too dearly, and I most certainly hold that the pleasure of those two hours' freshness is too dearly bought at the price of feeling languid and good for nothing all the rest of the day. This is the price they represent to me and to many others; but of course there are happy people who are made so strong that they can be up and out at sunrise without paying any heavy price for their pleasure—and instead of taunting their less fortunate fellow-creatures they should be thankful for their own superior strength.

Robert is one of the few people who, while getting up very early himself—generally at sunrise—yet by no means preaches the doctrine to others, but thinks that in that respect each should be a law to himself.

Most persons look upon early rising as a virtue in itself, and use it as an eminence from which to taunt others with laziness. They used to be most tyrannical and overbearing, but since doctors have lately taken the side of those who cannot stand early hours we do not hear so much of these early birds' crowing.

CHAPTER VII.

FERÓZPÚR, where we are now encamped, is on
the high bank of the old Ganges, overlooking
the wide flat stretch once covered by the river,
but deserted by it some hundreds of years ago
for a bed five miles eastward, and now covered
with thick grass jungle, groves of cocoa-nut
palms, and impenetrable reedy swamps.

This is where wild pig and hog-deer are
found, and where tigers live, but are *not* found ;
they only come out at night, and retire to their
swamps in the day. But, even setting aside the
swamps with their quicksands, there are deep,

narrow, broken ravines extending for miles along this high bank, covered with thorny jungle and absolutely impenetrable to anything but wild beasts ; so the tigers have every chance of living to a ripe age and dying finally in their beds. We hear that twenty-four bullocks were killed by them within three months last year.

This bank of the Ganges is studded all along with Hindu temples, which have fine flights of steps for bathers leading down to what used to be the river. Many of them are now deserted, and look very picturesque in their desolation, but other, perhaps more famous, shrines are still kept up and resorted to. I should think the priests must surely have looked upon the desertion of their shrines by the sacred river as a mark of their god's displeasure ; though, as theologians are always slow to allow anything that tells against their own views, perhaps these priests found some satisfactory solution for the conduct of the Ganges.

One evening we were returning along the low land very late, when we saw a curious sight

—thousands and thousands of crows going to roost amongst the tall reeds, which grow about sixteen feet high. We had often seen immense flights of crows flying eastward at dusk, but never knew whither they were bound ; now we saw them all assembled—from ten to twenty thousand, as far as we could guess—chattering like so many girls over their hair-brushing at night. Robert fired a shot to rouse them, when the whole swamp seemed to be converted into a noisy black mass, wheeling and darting in and out for a few minutes, after which they all subsided again into the forest of feathery reeds.

The Indian crows are not quite as big as rooks, but are very much like them in appearance and in their gregarious habits ; in England I found myself constantly calling the rooks crows—a terrible cockneyism in the eyes of those who only know the carrion crow, but very natural to any one acquainted with the Indian crows. These crows eat carrion, but they also eat fruit, and are altogether omnivorous ; a crow must not be critical about his dinner, or he may go to bed hungry. As a servant was taking away the luncheon things one day a crow swooped down and carried off a knife, in his haste mistaking the ivory handle for a bone. He was pursued for some distance, when, having discovered his mistake, he malignantly dropped the knife into a field of sugar-cane.

The crops this spring show splendid promise, and, if the weather continue favourable, prices ought to fall considerably in another month when the harvest begins. Just now they are terribly high, almost at famine height, and the people are sorely straitened. To give you an idea of the scarcity of grain, the corn called 'gram' (*Cicer arietinum*), which horses are fed on, was at *eighty-two pounds to the rupee* in the spring of 1876. It is now at *twenty-eight pounds*, and other grain and flour is in the same proportion. You can fancy that coolies' wages, four rupees a month, which enables them to live in tolerable comfort in a good year, is now barely enough to keep life in a man and his family. Poor things! their cheerfulness and patience are wonderful ; they will hardly complain till their bones come through their skins.

March 7.—Yesterday our cow was taken ill ; she refused to eat, and a great swelling came in her throat. The servants, full of faith, sent for the village medicine-man, who combines the characters of a holy man and a worker of magic. Thinking there is safety in numbers, our zealous bearer indeed summoned three of these wise men, who duly came and practised as follows. The first doctor gathered a twig of the Neem-tree (a wych-elm would perhaps answer in England), and with profound gravity stroked her throat with it for some time, muttering charms and incantations the while. The second heated an iron red-hot, and with it made a magic mark on the ground where her footprint was ; he also asked for a needle, and with it pierced her ear. The third made a ball of coarse sugar and caused a dog to lick it all over, after which the cow was made to swallow it. Proper prayers and charms having then been muttered over her, the wise men's work was over, and from that time the cow began to eat and is now getting well,—so scoff not at the means adopted. Are there not stranger things in heaven and earth than are dreamt of in our philosophy?

March 8.—At last the war-cloud that has so long been threatening to burst over Europe seems to be blowing over; to-day's telegrams announce the signing of the Treaty of Peace.[1] I was yesterday talking to my ayah about the war; my want of knowledge of the language crippled my eloquence sorely, and often obliged me to altogether forego saying something I should much wish to have said. She said many Mussulmans had left India to fight against the Russians, and wanted to know why we English did not fight them. I told her that many other nations were nearer the battle-field than we were, and that if other nations joined in whenever two had reason to fight there would be worse suffering and bloodshed than there is at present. I sounded her as to the feeling here with regard to the

---

[1] The treaty of San Stefano, between Russia and Turkey, signed March 3.

Russians; her sentiments are very unequivocal, and are, I suppose, a reflection of those around her. She says they long for the Russians to come to India, for that not one should leave it alive. I told her they were very fine soldiers, and that a thousand of them would beat 2,000 natives. 'If they would,' said the old woman fiercely, 'then they would not beat 10,000, and every man would leave his home, and his wife, and his children, and would go out to fight them.'

If this spirit is widespread the Russophobists may surely calm their fears. My ayah is not to be placed high as a politician, but as a reflector of public opinion in the bazaars she may be as good as many a wiser mouthpiece. I record her sentiments for what they are worth.

March 10.—The anniversary of the Prince of Wales's wedding-day in 1863, when I was at Mentone, and spent the morning in making bouquets of Neapolitan violets. How hot it was! And a feed was given to the Mentonese, and the band played 'God save the Queen,' and the gens d'armes had to go round and make the

men take off their hats, and as they did not put
them on again when the anthem was over
(having no idea why they had taken them off),
the gens d'armes had again to go round and
make them put them on. On two other occa-
sions only have I so distinct a recollection of the
playing of our National Anthem—once when
the Prince was at Lucknow, and it was played
to the accompaniment of the booming of the
Residency guns, on the very spot where our
people had suffered such agonies, and where our
hold on India had been so sorely tried ;—and
once when the Maharája of Bulrampur gave us
an entertainment, and it was played with im-
promptu variations and much cheerfulness on
instruments in every stage of tunelessness by his
own native band, while we drank sparkling
Moselle out of thick green-glass tumblers, and
nearly choked in our attempts to conceal our
amusement.

The new Order of the Crown of India has
been the subject of much criticism and attempted
witticism in the Indian papers.   One native
paper suggested gravely that an ' Order of the

Infant Empire' should be founded, 'to be re-
served for the grandchildren of Viceroys and
Governors, and for junior members of Council
and other distinguished personages.' This
borders on the profane, does it not? and it is
clear that the native mind is not yet educated up
to the point of appreciating stars and ribbons.
The last Order conferred lately on Scindia was
almost too much for him; he asks for his fortress of Gwalior, and they give him another star.
He was very sulky, and showed his ill-temper as
openly as he dared. It was very childish of him
not understanding the value of his new ribbon.

March 11.—On the march this morning a
native hunter we had with us shot a fine buck
antelope. When it was brought to me for orders
as to its disposal I inquired if it had been made
lawful' (*i.e.* for the Mahommedans, by having its
throat cut in the name of Allah). I was told it
was doubtful, as the hunter was a Hindu and had
no Mussulman with him, and, though he gave
his word that he had got a Mussulman to cut
its throat, still the matter could not be considered free from doubt. So not one of the

Mahommedans in our camp would eat of it, though their mouths watered to see such a fine fat buck.   One cannot but admire their genuine conscientiousness.

March 12.—We made a long march of seventeen miles into Meerut.   The bullock-carts which started over-night only reached our house at eight o'clock in the morning—an hour before we ourselves did—so half or more of the servants had been on the trudge all night.   They themselves take it so entirely as a matter of course that we fall into their views very kindly, and rarely give even a passing thought to the fact that our breakfast has been cooked by men who have been up and active almost the whole of the night.   Say I not truly that in spite of their faults they are excellent servants ?   If they were only as conscientious about speaking truth as they are about observing their ceremonial law they would be nearly perfect.   But after all, who can first throw a stone ?   Are there no Christians who think more of their ceremonial law and of observing their Sabbaths and assemblies than of doing justly, and loving mercy, and walking humbly with their God ?

March 20.—The weather is still very pleasant. On Saturday there was a great storm, accompanied unfortunately with hail, and much damage was done to the crops. The native habit of exaggeration makes it impossible to know what to believe ; we are told that stones fell weighing *three and four pounds*, killing much poultry and goats.

My visitors' list has now nearly eighty names on it, representing about 110 people. This, I dare say, will be an average number, but the individuals composing it are constantly changing—some go, others come. It is a very military station, the civil element being but a small part of the whole.

We are fortunate in having a rich and liberal landlord ; he is now building a rafter pitched roof over the present flat cement one, and is going to thatch it. This will make several degrees' difference in the heat, and will be a great boon. The compound is our weakest point ; it

is small, and when our ' at homes' begin, and we
have about fifty carriages (of sorts!) collected, I
hardly know where they will all put themselves.

March 24.—We are very anxious about poor
Mrs. Melville, who is, I fear, dying. Things
are so awfully sudden in India. On Tuesday
she had a tennis-party and was full of health,
and as bright and gay as usual. Wednesday
she was at the flower-show, but came away
early, not feeling well, and from that day there
has been slight hope. She was always the
picture of health, and able to undergo any
amount of exertion. How often I have envied
her health and strength ! So fair and young-
looking too, and kind and good. Every one
will grieve for her if, as we fear, she is taken.

Monday, March 25.—She died this morning,
and the funeral is to take place at sunrise to-
morrow—the day week of her tennis-party. We
do not need here in India to be reminded from
the pulpit that in the midst of life we are in
death. It is a thought almost always present.

March 27.—Robert and nearly everyone in

the station attended the funeral. The coffin was carried on a gun-carriage, and there was a party of sergeants both at the house and in the churchyard to help. All were anxious to show their sympathy.

Robert has received a telegram ordering him to take over charge as Officiating Judge from Mr. Melville, who is going home on furlough. The change of work will be pleasant during the hot season ; but a Judge does not go into camp, and I should miss that very much.

A high hot wind is blowing, and the whole air laden thickly with fine dust. Every door and cranny is carefully shut, but nevertheless the dust finds its way in and lays a thick deposit on everything.

I have made a splendid clove-orange, or rather lemon, for the Indian oranges wear such ridiculously loose jackets that they are of no use for this purpose. It has puzzled many people who said they never knew before how cloves grew !

April 4.—Our servants were away yesterday

at a great fair which is held annually near here. They returned with the news of a horrible thing which occurred during the day ; an elephant on which three Englishmen were riding was passing through the fair when he saw some sugar-cane being sold by a boy of twelve years old. He put out his trunk and helped himself to a bundle of it, and on the boy trying to snatch it from him he seized him with his trunk and crushed him to death under his foot. We have not yet heard it officially confirmed, but it is only too likely to be true. Elephants are very jealous and revengeful, and, like men, have sometimes horrible tempers ; considering their enormous size and strength, it is perhaps wonderful that on the whole they are as gentle and good-tempered as they are. I have seen an elephant ordered to kill a wounded boar, and it is a horrible sight ; he does not put his foot on the animal, but kicks it rapidly backwards and forwards once or twice between his hind and fore-foot. A Government elephant was sentenced to death the other day, after having killed ten men.

CHAPTER VIII.

April 9, 1878.—Is it to be war or peace ?
This is now the great topic of interest when two
or three people meet together. The mere pro-
spect of war has caused a blow to be dealt to all
military men which has produced infinite vexa-
tion and inconvenience. The leave season begins
in April, and half of the officers here, as else-
where, had long made their plans—some for
Kashmir, some for home, others for Simla, but
all for some holiday and to escape the heat of
the plains. Many had already given up their
bungalows and sold their horses, and some had

already started on furlough, while the others were busy with final preparations. In the midst of this an awful thunderbolt fell, in the shape of a simple telegram from the Commander-in-Chief: '*All leave stopped. Furlough already granted is cancelled*'—and the great exodus is arrested. You can imagine the dismay and confusion, the upsetting of plans, the wailing of the disappointed, the despair of those already gone at being recalled. One hope, however, inspires them all with tolerable resignation—surely this means war, and if so they are content. An officer was saying he believed that if we called for native volunteers we should have more at our disposal than we wished to send, so intense is their desire to fight the Russians. Meanwhile we live in suspense, and eagerly await the daily telegrams.

Other signs besides the leave season show us that the hot weather will soon be upon us. The Meerut hounds, as well as any valuable private dogs, are being sent up to the hills. Cartloads of favourite plants, such as geraniums,

are also being sent to spend the hot season at
Mussoorie, as they cannot stand the heat of the
plains. That will give you a practical idea of
what the heat is, as you know geraniums can
endure a heat that would make you wretched.
However, when it comes to a certain point the
geraniums die, and the human beings gasp, but
on the whole manage to live.

As yet the heat has not begun, there are only
signs of its beginning. At night the thermometer still goes down to 75°, so we have not yet
begun night-punkahs. After that we shall have
a month during which, with punkahs, we shall
sleep in tolerable comfort ; and then will come
a time when neither punkahs nor any human
invention will do anything more than mitigate
our suffering.

Never did I see such a place as this for flies
and mosquitoes. Flies we can destroy with the
fly-papers, and it is chiefly their ' vile corpuses '
that are offensive. But mosquitoes are wary,
they cannot be enticed, and there is no way of
getting rid of them. Robert says they make

such a roar when he draws the purdah of his dressing-room that he is afraid to go in alone!

Yesterday, as I was going into the spare room, a big rat jumped nearly on to me from out of the folds of the purdah, startling me horribly. Luckily my old cat was following me, and quickly she seized the rat by the crown and made an end of him.

April 17.—Great excitement among the military. The 9th Bengal Cavalry from here, and three other regiments from this division, have received orders to march on the 23rd for Bombay, but under sealed orders, so their destination is only guessed to be Russia. It is said that 50,000 native troops are to be sent in case of war. All the officers are wild with excitement, and packing up in case of receiving sudden marching orders.

April 20.—One of the advantages of India is the abundance of flowers. Many people, most indeed, who have no garden, still keep a gardener, and it is his business, naturally, to supply flowers every day and to arrange them. No one

asks where the flowers come from, it is enough
that there they are ; and so in every house you
see bowls and vases full of flowers worth
guineas in London.

We have a good garden, and a gardener who
has quite a talent for arranging flowers ; he sits
on his heels in the verandah on the north side
of the house, surrounded by mounds of roses of
every shade, but to-day chiefly creamy yellow
ones—petunias, myrtle, carnations, mignonette,
pomegranate, honeysuckle, big red lilies, scarlet
and white hibiscus, besides many flowers I never
saw except in India ; the beautiful tabernæmon-
tana with its waxy white clusters looking so
cool by the side of the flaming pomegranate, the
pale grey-blue plumbago, and, loveliest of all, the
feathery and graceful lagerströmia, with its large
tufts of white or purple or rose-coloured flowers.

April 29.—Punkahs yesterday in church for
the first time, and not before they were needed.
It is very amusing to observe their various
modes of swinging—some, hung by very long
ropes from the roof, swing with a long graceful

sweep ; others, hung underneath the gallery, go
with a short jerky swing very fussily ; while
the solitary one over the reading-desk went in
a most eccentric circle, waving all round the
Padre's head, and inviting speculation as to
whether or not it would fall foul of any other
punkah.

My meditations were further disturbed by
seeing what I took to be a monstrous rat
making swiftly for my petticoats ; I jumped up
and frightened him into turning back and darting
out, when I saw it was a squirrel. A lady behind me, who did not see that he had gone, was
in great agitation, sitting down and clasping
herself round the knees, till Robert turned round
and told her it had gone out, which reassured
her.

During week-day service lately there was
quite an exciting hunt in church ; one of the
many dogs who wait outside with the horses
and carriages, and never think of coming in
(though you must remember that there are about
ten large doors wide open on each side of the

church), suddenly saw a squirrel dart past him into the church. No right-minded dog could stand this, so in he chevyed, and a regular hunt ensued up and down and over the pews, the dog barking and the squirrel shrilly chattering.

These little episodes are inevitable in Indian life, and do not really attract as much attention as a bird does coming into an English church.

May 11.—The question of war as far from settled as ever. Meanwhile the Indian Contingent, numbering at present only 5,000 men or so, has sailed from Bombay. The Government orders were that the troops were to be embarked by a fixed date, and by dint of harassing the military executive to the verge of madness, the orders were carried out to the letter. Government was probably not informed of the trifling fact that a cavalry regiment was forced to embark before the ship was ready to receive them, *and before a drop of water was taken on board.* Zeal has its drawbacks. The cavalry officers were in despair, and the suffering endured must have been great. Fortunately the

troops were in the highest spirits, and inclined
to put up with a great deal. I do not know
what the horses felt—probably that the Yahoos
are only partly rational.

Last night quite a domestic tragedy was
enacted here ; a young deserted puppy that we
had found and adopted, and that was growing
up gay and light-hearted, was asleep with one of
the servants, when a wolf came. The puppy in
the stoutness of his heart got up and defied him
loudly, but alas ! the wolf seized him and tore
him so cruelly that the poor puppy shortly died.
His shrieks were heartrending. Poor puppy !

Bulandshahr, May 13.— This is a station
about forty miles south of Meerut, and Robert
has to hold a week's sessions here. We had five
pairs of horses laid for us, and as the road is
metalled the whole way we came very pleasantly
in our own carriage, starting yesterday soon
after five o'clock in the afternoon, and getting
here at eleven, having halted for half an hour
half-way to eat our dinner. It tasted very good
by the light of the moon, and luckily we finished

our last jam puff before we got caught in a dust storm, which half suffocated us, and filled our mouths, eyes, and ears with sand.

On arriving here we found some of the servants, who had started the night before in a camel carriage—such a thing ! looking like a wild beasts' cage on wheels, having iron bars all round, and a thatch at top, and being drawn by a camel.

The rest of the servants arrived this morning; we brought as few as we could manage with, and find they come to *nineteen* ! We have had a good bungalow lent us, and as it has punkahs, and we have coolies to pull them, we are indifferent to the exceeding scarcity of chairs and other luxuries. I forgot to bring a footstool, and so told the bearer he must have one of some sort contrived. Next day one was brought—you should see it ! It is a little table, so long and high, but it supports my feet till I move them, when its legs come out. It is original, but hardly a success.

Meerut, May 23.—You may like to see a

sketch of a fruit-tree after being pruned according to native ideas. It was a shady spreading
tree, in full leaf, and Robert in going round
the garden suggested that it took up too much
space, and would be the better for pruning.
' Yes,' responded the gardener cheerfully, ' if
the order be given it shall be pruned.' ' Do so,'
said Robert, and next morning he beheld the
result. Not a leaf or a twig was left to mourn
for its fellows,—all alike had gone, and the
thick boughs had been sawn off very neatly at
the first fork made by each. There was no
doubt it had been pruned, and the gardener was
quite satisfied with his morning's work.

We are having most abnormal weather, the
temperature being 7° lower than has been known
in May for twenty-five years. It is very pleasant, but, like so many pleasant things, very un-
wholesome. There is much severe sickness
amongst the troops here, and at Morar and
Bareilly there is a frightful outbreak of cholera;
thirty deaths already out of forty-five Europeans
attacked, and nearly fifty deaths per cent. among

the natives attacked. We tremble lest it should come here. Meanwhile the world plays tennis and keeps up its spirits.

Prices are now nearly at famine rates, and the mortality among the people is enormously in excess of the average, partly from actual starvation, but still more from weakness and sickness consequent on insufficient food.

Some people think that our Government in its resolve to save life is but pitting its strength against Nature's, and that, inasmuch as Providence is stronger than even the English Government, it will sooner or later baffle its devices for saving superfluous life, and will again reduce the population of India by famine or pestilence to its normal limits. It is certain that fifty millions can live in comfort in an area where, if you insist on rearing one hundred millions, life becomes a bare struggle for existence. Terrible, therefore, as is a famine, it doubtless makes more room for those who are left, and it seems to be Nature's way of adjusting the balance between food and population.

We finite creatures cannot judge the matter from the standpoint of an infinite wisdom, nor are we taken into the counsels of the Almighty. We only grope along dimly in such light as we have, and it may be that some of our wisest and most philanthropic schemes are only so much kicking against the pricks, so much struggling against a scheme too great and wide for our intelligence.

Still we can only act according to our light, and that undoubtedly prompts us to save human life when we can. We should be less than human if we did not. But it does not follow that were we *more* than human we should act the same. Can we not imagine what a matter of absolute unimportance it must seem to the 'eternal hills,' the Himalayas, whether so many millions of human insects die fifty years sooner or later? Die they must, and if by dying now any benefit is conferred on the great majority who survive, why not die?

June 4.—Going to bed in India is such a very different process from going to bed in

England, that I must bring the difference before you. To begin with, it is a far less formal process. There is (in the hot season) no shutting of the door, no cutting yourself off from the outer world, no going upstairs, and finally no getting into bed. You merely lie down on your bed, which with its bedding is so simple as to be worth describing. The bed is a wooden frame with webbing laced across it, and each bed has a thin cotton mattrass. Over this one sheet is spread, and two pillows go to each bed, bolsters not being used. *Voilà tout!* Some people do not even have the mattrass, preferring the coolness of a piece of fine matting. Across the two beds hangs the punkah, with a great quilted towel hung on to it so low as nearly to sweep our faces and keep mosquitoes off; it is very nice when once you are down, but highly enraging as it flaps your head first on one side and then on the other before you can lie down.

Our room is a cube of twenty feet as near as may be, so we have quite the required hospital

number of cubic feet of air to breathe! Besides
which it has four large doors, all of which stand
permanently open, with only a chintz purdah
across the lower part. This chintz purdah is
all that divides you from the punkah coolies in
the verandah and the world at large. The bedroom is purely a sleeping-room ; we each have a
dressing-room and bath-room besides.

June 15.—I wish some of the good people
who talk at home of its being ' positively Indian
heat' when the thermometer goes up to 90° for
a few hours could come now on a week's visit to
us. It would wonderfully enlighten their minds
or freshen their memories as to what Indian
heat is, and might prevent their talking so
wildly of ' positively Indian heat.'

Every one who has been in India, and also in
Africa and Australia, knows that, owing to some
peculiarity of the atmosphere, heat is felt very
much more in India than the same degree of
heat in Australia would be. Of this there is
sufficient proof in the fact that, although the
thermometer sometimes goes as high in Australia

as it does here, yet the country can be colonised by Englishmen, nor are punkahs or tatties required to keep people or dogs alive. Whereas it has always been impossible to colonise the plains of India, as the second generation, or so many as survive childhood, are weak miserable creatures, destroyed in body and mind by the heat.

The heat, therefore, registered by the thermometer does not convey an accurate idea of the heat and suffering felt, and allowance must always be made for this. But here are a few facts, taken from the Allahabad weather report, for you to bear in mind when next you hear any one comparing English heat with Indian :—
'For the last week in May the register showed never less than 105° as the maximum temperature *in the shade.* June opened with *110°.* The figures rose steadily day by day until on the 7th *117°* was reached. For three days in succession *116°* was registered, and the thermometer is now (June 14) stationary at *113°.* The maximum temperature in the sun's rays

was 168°. The minimum registered at four o'clock A.M. on the 11th was 93°.'

The excessive dryness of the air—sometimes the humidity being as low as 8° out of a possible 100°—makes it feel like the blast of a furnace ; it heats any ironwork, in the shade, till you can hardly bear your hand on it, and it heats the bath-towels till they make me gasp as I dry my face!

Everything possible is done to keep our house cool. It is almost hermetically closed, and only thrown open during the coolest hours of the night. But though in this way we keep it down to 92° in the day, we cannot get it cooler even at night ; and that is what makes it so wearing, that you *never* get any respite from the heat. The deaths from heat apoplexy have been many, but that is the case every year. At the great railway stations they have coffins in readiness for the dead bodies which are sure to be found daily in the trains, dead not from sun heat, but from sheer air heat.

My head often feels as if it were being fried,

and all night long I keep it and my pillows well sopped with cold water.

We are having a punkah rigged up out of doors, and mean to dine and sit out of doors at night, as the temperature is always some degrees lower then in the open than in the house. You, thinking of a hot English summer night, will think how delightfully cool and pleasant it must be, but I can assure you it is only mitigated misery ; the thermometer stands at 100°.

CHAPTER IX.

SUDDEN DEATH—FLIGHT OF LOCUSTS—DUST-STORMS—WHITE
ANTS—BABY A MONTH OLD—HIS DHAIE—FALL OF FISH
—ZOOLOGICAL STAKES—GRASS-CUTTERS' PONIES.

June 23.—Thank Heaven! a change has come. All Friday and yesterday the atmosphere was tawny and thick with dust, and the heat frightful. Towards evening the air became still thicker and tawnier, till there was a kind of awful oppression and sense of something impending. Then in a moment the trees swayed and bowed their heads, a furious wind came sweeping by, it changed suddenly to the east, and instantly the relief was felt. The burning blast from the west was gone.

The night set in with heavy clouds, and before morning we had a storm of rain, and woke to-day to see a grey sky, all the doors open, and the thermometer down to 86°. You can hardly understand the intense relief. We hope it is the setting in of the monsoon, but cannot tell yet. Anything is a relief from that intolerable burning heat ; but the exchange is only to a *stewing* heat for the next three months at best—a perpetual Turkish bath, which makes the skin soft, and brings prickly heat to torment one with its sharp stabs and pricks.

June 26.—We have just had another practical sermon on the words ' In the midst of life we are in death.' It would be strange if we did not remember them. At the band-stand last night, where every one was assembled, the Riding Master of the Artillery was seized with heat apoplexy. He was taken away by two doctors, and we hear he never spoke again. This afternoon a notice has come round to say his funeral takes place this evening. Riding to the band one night—carried to the cemetery the next. Such is Indian life.

June 28.—Yesterday evening a cloud of locusts suddenly made its appearance, coming from the north, and darkening the air as it came. It is a wonderful sight anywhere, but not nearly as striking on the plains as when seen in the hills, as then you can form a better idea of the vastness of the flight. You see valleys 2,000 feet below you filled with the fluttering wings, you yourself are nearly blinded by the whirling mass of insects round you, and you look up and see mountain-tops 3,000 feet above you encircled by reddish clouds, still of locusts.

Here you lose much of this effect. You can only see that the whole sky above you is darkened by the fluttering host, and that as far as the eye can reach the air is thick with them, looking like snowflakes where the sunlight falls on them, and like dark red spots where they come between the sun and you.

A tremendous hullabaloo was set up by all the people about the place to prevent them from settling here, and where any did alight they were screamed at and stoned till they rose again and fluttered further. They *must* settle somewhere for the night, but woe betide the hapless spot where they alight. They have jaws like horses, and appetites like ogres. We shall, no doubt, trace their course through the newspapers, which never fail to chronicle such 'fashionable arrivals.'

June 29.—No rain, nor sign of it, but an abominable dust-storm in the evening, which caught us when out driving. We noticed a very lurid ominous light on a heavy bank of clouds, but thought we should have time to get home. Five minutes later we saw the vultures and kites swooping about in great disorder, evidently beating up against a wind that had not yet reached us, and then we knew the storm was on us. In another moment the first gust of cold wind had struck us, and we were in the midst of a dense pall of dust, and darkness so great that we had to pull up and stand still until the worst of the storm was past. The coachman and syces were sorely exercised about their hats, which are much the shape and size of bread-platters, and offer a good surface to the wind.

I must say these Meerut dust-storms are great impostors; they look most awful as they approach, but when they come are never very bad, never at all equalling those we had in Oudh, where a man once left our house just as one was coming on, and twenty minutes later came knocking at the windows for admittance, having been unable till then either to find his way out of the compound or back to the house!

July 9.—Joy at last! The rains seem really to have set in, and four inches have fallen in the last two days. The frogs are having a perfect jubilee; there are two sets of them apparently, and they sing antiphonal chants all the evening, each set letting the other have its turn in the fairest manner. What they have done with themselves all through the hot weather I do not know, no one sees or hears them, but the moment the rains begin they swarm. The sweeper goes round the house and collects a water-can full of juveniles every evening, and deports them to a distance. Another rain creature that appears with the toad tribe is a lovely red velvet insect about the size of a huge lady-bird. He is exactly like a button of softest crimson velvet. The natives believe he is rained from the sky.

Swarms of white ants, too, begin to emerge from unsuspected underground galleries, all in the brief enjoyment of four immense wings, which wings seem to be as badly put on as were those of Icarus, for they drop off all over the rooms, till wafted into drifts by the punkah, and then the wretched ants wriggle about as grubs until eaten up or swept away. They are quite harmless in this stage, having got through all their books, boots, carpets, and so on before coming out in the glory of wings.

July 13.—The monsoon has fairly set in all over India, and fears of a famine are for the present at an end. The people are beginning to sow their land, and thousands will now find work who up to the present have only been saved from starvation by the Government relief works. The servants, too, are in great spirits at the fall in the price of grain ; when your whole income is 10s. a month, it makes an appreciable

difference whether flour is thirty or forty lbs. to
the rupee.

.   .   .   .   .   .

Aug. 17.—The baby a month old, and as
big as a native child three times his age. We
have a dhaie, a native wet-nurse, for him, but
were afraid we should have to part with her, as
her husband is a most violent-tempered man,
and after she had been a week with us came
vowing she should not stop, and that he would
hang himself unless she returned home. Considering that she had come with his full consent,
this conduct on his part was very ' contumacious
and indecent,' as Mrs. Proudie would express it.
However, we at once looked out for another
dhaie, and when he found that we had taken
him at his word, he repented him, and thought
of the rupees he was throwing away ; and this so
worked on him that he came to tender his abject
submission, and agreed to sign a paper in which
he promised not to interfere with his wife as
long as we require her services.

She is a regular villager, of bucolic intelli- .
gence, but improving. She has lately begun to

notice the various strange ornaments and furniture, and even ask simple questions.   I pointed
out a large print of Herring's three horses' heads,
and asked her what animals they were.   She
studied them attentively for some time, and then
said, ' Perhaps they were camels.'   You must
remember that never in her life had she seen a
picture, which is a state of mind we are hardly
able to realize.   Most of the servants in hanging
a picture would hang it upside down, so little
can they see any meaning in it.   I suppose it
is chiefly a matter of education.   I wonder if a
dog could be taught to recognize a portrait ?

We have had no rain for a month except
two showers, and the heat has been horrible,
ranging only from 94° to 87° indoors night and
day.   One sign, however, by which we may
know that this is, according to the calendar, the
rainy season, is the sociable way in which the
toads give us their company.   Big and little,
they like to have a house over their heads at
this season, and they find ours convenient.
During the day they do not show, and only

sing their little cheerful quavering song in retired corners of the drawing-room ; but no sooner are the lamps lighted than out they hop in family processions. Their worst enemy is the white kitten, who hunts them about with merciless energy and many hard pats.

Aug. 20.—A most singular phenomenon occurred to-day. Heavy rain had been falling, and a perfect stream was rushing out from our compound by an outlet near the stables. Suddenly a large shoal of little fish was noticed in the shallow water, and the servants turned out with sticks and baskets and killed and caught four pounds' weight of them. The Kitmatgár caught one which he declares he *saw* fall from the air, and brought it to Robert, who weighed it and found it to weigh one ounce. Another man says he was standing under a tree when he saw a fish fall from the branches, and tried to catch it, but lost it in the grass. Now, our compound has no water in it, nor any hollow where water can lie, nor is there any inlet for water ; the whole compound being enclosed by a bank and low wall, with only the carriage gate at the upper end, and an outlet for flood water at the *lower* end, towards which the fish were being swept by the stream from the garden. Therefore the question arises, Where did these fish come from if not from above? Such a phenomenon eighteen centuries ago would have been a miracle. If it is not one now, what then is required to constitute a miracle? Could anything be called a miracle in these days of newspapers, telegraphs, and scientific men? or would not a solution be offered of any phenomenon? I merely record the facts, an account of which we have sent to the newspaper. I am by no means prepared to defend the theory of the fish having fallen from the clouds, but at the same time I have no other conceivable theory to suggest. Fish are not likely to have jumped over the wall in any numbers, even if any chance had brought them to the other side of it.

The heat continues frightful. Ten days ago an officer left here invalided for England; sleep was of the utmost importance to him in his weak state, but it appears that the guards all along the line had received orders to wake any passengers who appeared to be asleep, for fear they should in reality be dead or dying from heat apoplexy, so fearfully numerous have the deaths been. So the poor fellow was constantly roused from sleep during the weary journey of three days and three nights to Bombay.

So many people are away at the hills that Meerut seems perfectly deserted. I think there are only nine ladies now here, no garden parties or entertainments, and one expects to see the Mall grass-grown.

The only rendezvous now is on Thursdays, when there are public sports and races, tent-pegging, riding at the ring, and so on. One of the 'events' one week was the following :—

'ZOOLOGICAL STAKES.

'A HANDICAP FOR ALL ANIMALS EXCEPT HORSES, MULES, PONIES, OR DONKEYS. ANIMALS NOT SUITED FOR RIDING MAY BE ACCOMPANIED BY THEIR OWNERS ON FOOT.'

Among the entries were a bullock, a mongoose, a camel, a partridge, and some deer! The partridge came in first. Then there was a race for grass-cutters' ponies, very amusing. These ponies are accustomed to go out every morning to fetch grass, returning in the evening with no part of them visible but a head and legs, the rest wholly eclipsed by two enormous bundles of grass. They invariably go in a long string, one after another. Now, on the racecourse was a hurdle-jump. At the start one pony got well away from the others till he came to the hurdles, when he swerved and went outside. Mark the force of habit! Every other pony in the race, in spite of all efforts of their riders, followed suit and tailed off in single file after their leader.

There is a belief at home, which I used to share, that horses cannot walk as camels do, moving the fore and hind leg of the same side at the same time. But this belief is speedily uprooted on reaching India. Ponies are especially taught this peculiar gait, which is called 'kadam' or 'step,' and is much liked by the natives. Some people think it is what is meant by 'ambling.' It is taught by tying the fore and hind foot together at the proper distance.

CHAPTER X.

DRIVE TO BULANDSHAHR—MR. GROWSE AND HIS WORKMEN—
COMMON SIGHTS ON AN INDIAN ROAD—FLOODS IN PUN-
JÁB—KITTEN AND MANTIS—WAGES' LIST—SEPARATION OF
JUDICIAL AND ADMINISTRATIVE BRANCHES—AVERAGE OF
TEMPERATURE FOR FIVE MONTHS—KID STAKES—PINK
POODLE — GRASS-CUTTERS — NECESSITY OF GOVERNMENT
TAKING UP LAND—CABUL MISSION TURNED BACK.

Bulandshahr, Aug. 26.—We came over here
yesterday, accomplishing the journey without
any excitement till the last stage, and then we
had a pair of brutes that would not start. They
backed violently, at the same time turning
round, so that one of them brought his haunches
right against the carriage-door, bending the
handle, and narrowly escaping upsetting the
carriage. They were got straight and we tried
to start once more, but they repeated their per-

formance more viciously than ever, so that we both of us jumped nimbly out, thinking the carriage must be pushed over. The coachman assured us that if once they started they went like the wind, and he persuaded us to give them one more trial, he at their heads and our last coachman (for a coachman stays with his own horses) on the box to drive them. One or two furious whacks and pushes, and they really did start, at a gallop, but straight along the road. Then their coachman clambered on to the box— how, I cannot think—and a wrathful struggle for the reins ensued between him and the other driver, intensified by the fact that it is the *driver* who gets a tip.

It reminded me strongly of a ludicrous struggle I once saw take place in a pulpit—one of the old three-decker pulpits of the past. The clerk was lighting the candles, when the rector, who was both absent-minded and short-sighted, walked up into the pulpit and so hemmed him in. The pulpit being small, the clerk had not room to pass, and the rector had not the presence of mind to retreat. A regular struggle ensued, till at last the clerk, in a frenzy, took the rector by the shoulders, whirled past him, and fled at one bound down the stairs, leaving the rector in sole possession, flustered and fiery.

Aug. 31.—On Thursday we dined with the Collector here, who is a man of antiquarian propensities, an encourager of native art, and truly a 'collector' of things of beauty and value. He keeps various silversmiths and other artisans at work in his compound. Just now he is having a reredos made which is intended to adorn a church in Suffolk, and will surely be unique of its kind. It is of Mainpúri work, which is wood inlaid with delicate brass wire, and two workmen have been employed on it for some months and have about half finished it. As in all Indian work, the instruments are of the simplest. The men were sitting—*all* Indian work is done sitting on the ground—under a thatched lean-to, each with a portion of the reredos between his knees. The work is very simple, but infinitely tedious. First the design is drawn in pencil, generally an exquisitely graceful and elaborate arabesque with curves of many centres. This is then cut into the wood with a very small chisel, after which fine brass ribbon wire is hammered in. The effect is very delicate and beautiful.

The days are shortening now very perceptibly, to our comfort, as the sun has not so much time to heat the air before he is obliged to ' move on.' It is a strange thought that, if we could look at the world from a great distance, there would be no such thing to be seen as alternate day and night. It would be one incessant and simultaneous sunrise, noon, and sunset, one merging into the other as the colours do in the rainbow. The idea of morning and evening making up a day is clearly a local one, emanating from a being who can only be in one place at once, and cannot follow the sunrise as it travels round the world.

Meerut, Sept. 2.—We returned yesterday, and were very lucky in our day. Heavy rain must have fallen somewhere, and had cooled the air delightfully. Our long drive of forty miles was most enjoyable, the country looking exquisitely green, and the ground covered with crops—indigo, cotton, sugar-cane, maize, and jowár—all looking flourishing.

For a great part of the way the road is lined with fine Babúl-trees (the shittim-wood of the Bible, I believe), which are now covered with their powdery yellow little balls of blossom, filling the air with a faint scent. There was a great deal of water out, and for a long distance the trees were standing in it, their clear reflections looking very pretty ; the low western sun was throwing a most lovely light on their trunks, while the shadow side was peculiarly black and soft. The common sights along an Indian road, too, are always picturesque—the wide plains, with great herds of smoke-coloured, delicate-limbed cattle being driven slowly home for the night, accompanied by troops of ungainly, fierce-looking buffaloes, and flocks of goats and black long-tailed sheep. Then gangs of wayfarers clad in every colour and degree of costume, from the simple suit of ashes of the Fakír to the gorgeous combination of white and coloured raiment of some rich man who has just dismounted hurriedly from his carriage, drawn by a pair of white humped oxen, to salaam to Robert. Some of the men we met had rather a fiendish look, their whole bodies as well as their scanty garments being of a dark hideous blue colour ; they were men employed in indigo-making, which at this time of the year is in full swing.

Wherever we stopped to change horses a crowd gathered round us, gazing at us as silently and respectfully as a herd of cattle, but much more picturesque to look at. One dear fat little girl about four years old had nothing on but a cap—but the cap was very fine.

Then you come to a pond, where some buffaloes are enjoying themselves immensely, with no part of them visible but the tips of their noses ; while on the bank is a group of children very merry over washing their clothes (a waist-

cloth forming the full suit), which they are fluttering in the wind to dry, while they run about
meanwhile perfectly and happily naked.

Further on some men are ploughing in a
field, two to plough and three to look on ; but as
we pass they all stand still to look at us, oxen
and all.

Then you pass a group of travellers making
a halt, all sitting in a circle by the road smok-
ing by turns the friendly hookah. Presently
a perfect caravan of those quaint two-storied
camel carriages, so like a travelling menagerie ;
then a long line of country carts creaking slowly
along, laden with indigo-pulp.

Under a tree we saw a dead camel stretched
out, looking even more leggy and angular in
death than in life.

There was always something to attract one's
attention, and make reading out of the question.
I think it was Charles Lamb who said he did
not *believe* in reading out of doors ; I quite share
his disbelief.

The sun set in a flood of gold light, with a few long low bars of intensely black cloud to emphasize the brilliant beauty of the colouring, and by the time we reached home it was quite dark but for a young moon.

This is certainly a luckless country. After suffering grievously from drought it gets rain, but more in anger than in kindness apparently. The floods in the Punjáb have been widespread and most destructive to crops, cattle, property, and life. The river Bayne, a small stream usually thirty yards across, is now an immense volume of water two miles in breadth, and flowing with a velocity equal to the Sutlej. Several railway-bridges have given way, and there is an interruption of traffic for more than thirty miles.

Sept. 4.—Yesterday evening the kitten had been playing about for a long while without our particularly noticing her, but at last I looked to see what she was playing with, and found it was a large praying mantis ; it was a charming plaything, as it can run very fast, and when it stopped she gave it a pat to make it go on, or took it in her mouth and tossed it up. This game had been long going on before I saw and rescued the mantis ; but, wonderful to say, she had not hurt it in the least, at least not visibly. I dare say if the truth were known his bones are aching somewhat, but bruises would not show, as he could not be greener than he is.

You might like to see a list of our servants and their wages, so I will copy a page of my wages' book. This is our hot season list ; in the camping season we do not have punkah-coolies, but their place is taken by others who run out with our daily *dáli* of bread, eggs, mutton, and vegetables. We then also have four or five tent-pitchers and a tribe of camel and bullock drivers, elephant drivers, and other miscellaneous camp followers. Most of them, however, are paid by Government, and I will only give you a list of our own private servants. Besides them, Robert has five chuprassies, or orderlies, in attendance, but they are Government servants :—

Name of Servant	Best English equivalent	Monthly Wages Rupees
Khansáma	Butler	10
Kitmatgár	Footman	8
Bawarchi	Cook	10
Masálchi	Scullion	5
Bearer	Valet, &c.	10
Mate-bearer	Assistant do.	6
Ayah	Lady's-maid	10
Dhaie	Wet-nurse	10
Mehteráni	Low-caste ayah	4
Mehter	Sweeper	5
Dhobi	Washerman	13
Bhisti	Water-carrier	5
Derzie	Tailor	10
Murghiwalla	Fowl-keeper	5
Goála	Cowman	5
Chokidar	Watchman	5
Coachwán	Coachman	8
3 Syces	Grooms	15
3 Grass-cutters		12
6 Punkah-coolies		24
2 Garden-coolies		8
Máli	Gardener	6

Total, 32 servants. Total monthly wages Rs. 194

Small as the wages are, the total amounts yearly to 2,328 Rs., or 232*l.* 4*s.* But this includes nearly the whole cost of the servants, for you must remember they feed themselves. The only one we feed is the dhaie, who is thereby put out of caste, and has to pay a fine to be readmitted to caste privileges on leaving our service. We also give a suit of warm clothes in the winter to the coachman and half a dozen others, but that only costs a few rupees a head, and generally lasts two cold seasons.

For this cost you could hardly keep five servants at home, and, however good those five might be, their goodness would not extend to being in thirty-two places at once. So that on the whole you get far more comfort from your Indian than from your English servants.

India would simply be intolerable with only five servants, and those five with English ideas and ways. I am only speaking of the *average* servants of both countries ; and I do not say that any Indian servant can equal a thoroughly excellent, devoted, well-educated English one, for, owing to the different national characteristics, I think they hardly could. It is not that these are less faithful or devoted, for as a rule they are far more so, and many an ayah in the Mutiny proved her devotion at the cost of her life, and many would do so again. But there is not the same high moral standard, especially with regard to truth ; and this is where a first-rate Indian servant would stand a step lower than a first-rate English one. In fact, the conclusion I have come to is that an individual English servant may be more valuable than an individual here can be, but that the average servants here are better than the average at home.

Sept. 7. — We heard yesterday of Mr. C——'s death from fever at Agra. It must have been very sudden, as no one had heard of his being ill. He is another victim to the weakness men have for staying on too long in India ; his health was not good, and he should have retired when he had served his time. He hoped, of course, to get into the High Court. He has now gone to the highest court—but not as judge.

Robert has received a Government circular, announcing that with a view to relieving the block now existing in promotion it has been decided to separate the administrative and judicial branches of the service, and officers are requested to elect which line they would prefer. Robert has elected for the judicial line, promotion in which leads to the High Court ; but, as he has every intention of retiring in four years' time, he is not likely to rise so high. Nature assumes that he will, for she supposes that all High Court judges need wigs, and she is gradually preparing him with a suitable head for wearing one. However, wigs are not *de rigueur* in India—and wisely, for if they were the inclination would be too strong to sit in your wig and nothing else.

Yesterday, on moving a clothes-basket, it was found that the white ants had made an irruption in the night and had impartially eaten the bottom of the basket and sundry linen garments. We made a libation of petroleum and removed the basket. Last night they came up again, and must have been disappointed to find the basket and clothes gone.

Sept. 13.—This morning I struck the average of the readings of our self-registering thermometer in the drawing-room for the last five months, and find that from April 1 to

August 31 the average *maximum* is 86° and the average *minimum* 80°. The mean temperature, therefore, of the last five months indoors has been 83°.

This may be depended on as accurate, for, knowing how greatly thermometers vary, I sent ours to the Meteorological Reporter to be tested by a standard thermometer. Ours was found to mark two degrees too low, so all my readings are corrected ones.

Some people really like having a thermometer that marks very low, as they like to say that they can keep *their* house down to 90° when every one else has it at 94°. They would not for the world have it tested !

Sept. 14.—At the athletic sports yesterday (called the Gymkhána. You ask why ? I also ask why ? and Echo and all my neighbours answer why ?) there was one race called the Kid Stakes, for sons of soldiers, handicapped according to age. One dear little gunner of five was entered ; but his handicap availed him little, as he did not think of starting till the others had

overtaken him, but then set off manfully, pound-
ing away on his sturdy little legs most conscien-
tiously up to the winning-post. I should so
like to have improvised a prize for him, but,
owing to the Indian custom of one's bearer
keeping all the money, our pockets were
empty.

The only other point of interest was a pink
poodle. At first I took him to be a carriage-
mat on the ground, but presently he moved,
and I saw he was a curly poodle dyed bright
pink all over. The effect was decidedly striking.

Sept. 19.—We are looking forward greatly
to a trip to the hills during the Judges' Vaca-
tion, which begins next week, when the Courts
are closed for a month.

Yesterday a pony was sent for me to look
at, and, as we like the looks of him, we have
bought him, and started him off this morning in
care of a syce and grass-cutter to Rájpúr, at the
foot of the Mussoorie hills. It will take the
men about a week to march there, which will.

bring him up in time for me to ride up the hill next Thursday, I hope.

There is an odd custom in India, that when you sell a horse you give in with him his blanket and perhaps an old suit of clothing, his head and heel ropes, surcingle, and watering bridle, and the coachman yesterday was rather aggrieved because no watering-pail had been sent as well!

The animal's syce and grass-cutter are generally also sent with him, and are usually taken on by his new master. This pony's grass-cutter, however, objected to go to the hills; he was also a bad servant, for he said he would only bring in 24 lbs. of grass a day, and the common allowance to each horse daily is 50 lbs. It is a curious arrangement, for the men are supposed to get it where they can, and in the hot season, when grass is scarce, they have to go great distances to get the required amount. It leads also to ill-feeling between them and the villagers, whose rights it certainly entrenches on. The grass-cutters belonging to the cavalry regi-

ments go out in perfect squadrons, and not un-
frequently there are regular fights between them
and the villagers. The necessity is now being
discussed of Government taking up sufficient
land in the neighbourhood of its cantonments to
supply the necessary grass. It is great injustice
that this should not have been done long ago, as
the value of the grass required every day is something enormous, and in hard seasons, when
fodder is scarce, the villagers need it all for their
cattle. Government will have to take some such
step before long, and I wonder that none of the
Indian agitators at home have called the attention of Parliament to this particular blot. I
wonder if it could be made into a party
matter !

Sept. 25.—Exciting news from the frontier—
that the Ameer's commandant has flatly refused
to let the Mission pass. It has therefore had to
retire, and the dogs of war seem likely to be let
loose. The 60th Rifles and several batteries of
artillery have received orders for active service,
and all the officers are in a state of delighted

excitement. I do not understand Cábul politics, nor, I think, do most people, but a young artillery officer yesterday put the present popular feeling on the subject into a nutshell. He said to me, ' I know nothing of politics, but I know that if a nigger cheeks us we must lick him.'

The popular feeling could not be more concisely stated, or in language more free from pedantry.

CHAPTER XI.

Rájpúr, Sept. 26.—Here we are at the foot of
the hills, and sitting without punkahs. We left
Meerut yesterday by the afternoon train and
had a three hours' journey to Sahâranpúr. The
country very flat and monotonous, the only
pretty thing being the wide stretches of flowering grass, with its snow-white feathery tufts like
the pampas. At Sahâranpúr we dined at the
railway *table d'hôte*; dishes there were many,
of varying degrees of badness, and we ate of the
very fellow to Dr. Johnson's famous *gigot*—as
bad as bad could be, ill fed, ill killed, and ill
cooked ; at least we tried to eat it, but failing,

we asked if there was any pudding. ' No pudding,'
said the man, ' but jelly.' Thinks I to myself,
what a purist to object to jelly being classed as
pudding ; however, said I, ' Give me some jelly.'
In a moment or two the servant returned with
a *jam dish*! and offering it to me said, ' It is
currant jelly '! This was a disappointment.

Dinner finished, we got into the omnibus we
had chartered to take our whole party the forty
miles to Rájpúr. You must disabuse your mind
of *all* notions of any omnibus you ever saw. It
has no seats, only a flooring of boards, under
which our luggage was stowed, and over which
we spread our thin mattresses, and then packed
ourselves in a row, heads and tails, like wine-
bottles.

The shaking was something awful. Being
dark, we could not see what caused it, but at
times it felt as if we were leaping over a succession of paved gutters. We had hung up our
lantern to a bar at the top, and moored it below ;
but the shocks to its system were too much, its
top came bodily off, and the lower part fell,

narrowly missing the boy's innocent upturned face.

During the night we crossed the range of low hills into the enclosed plain of Dehra Doon, having sometimes bullocks and sometimes extra horses, but we were half asleep all the time, and did not know much of what went on.

We got in here at six o'clock this morning, and shall ride up the hill, 7,000 feet, this afternoon. It is pleasant to see great bushes of scarlet geraniums here ; they tell of a different climate from our Meerut furnace.

Sept. 27.—We started the boy and the servants off early in the afternoon, and ourselves followed an hour or so later, Robert on a hired pony, and I on the one bought last week. The first three miles are frightfully steep, and one has to hang on to the pony's mane to take the strain off one's back a little. We met long strings of pack-mules and ponies, who come down laden with potatoes, and take return loads of wheat. It was delightful to see once more the hills and banks covered with ferns and wild flowers, and to smell the pleasant *earthy* smell of a cool climate again. Wild dahlias grow in masses near Mussoorie ; they are small and of course single, but of brilliant colours, and grow in thick tangled masses down the steep hillsides.

We overtook the advance guard two miles from Mussoorie, and our boxes even sooner, so we had nothing up with us when we reached the hotel, having got up in exactly two hours. *Table d'hôte* was at 7.30, and I had to appear in my riding-habit for lack of anything else. Such a curious set of people at table, and such curious English to be heard ; a few ladies (save the mark !) looking and behaving as much like barmaids as they could. The influence of fashionable manners in high places is not happy in its effect on the manners of those who are *not* in high places, however faithful they may try to make the imitation.

We are settled in very pleasant south rooms, the mountain-side stretching away from our hotel right down to the plains, which lie like a map spread out before us, the towns of Rájpúr and Dehra looking like white specks on it.

This is the most lovely month in the hills— the rains over, and a fresh bright feeling in the air like a glorious September day in Scotland.

The English papers are assuming a most warlike tone, and threatening the Viceroy with every editor's indignation should he refuse to march on Cábul instantly. They seem to think that crossing the frontier and opening a campaign in Affghánistán is like sending an army into Wales, and can be undertaken as promptly. It is very nice for the Viceroy having the proper course of action decided for him, but it takes off from the value of advice when the givers of it are irresponsible for consequences.

Oct. 7.—Yesterday we took a long walk— *i.e.* Robert on his pony, and I in a dandy, a kind of canoe-shaped seat carried on two men's shoulders. Coming home, Robert by way of experiment took the place of one of my coolies, but did not move two steps before calling for the man to relieve him, who grinned as he resumed

his place and trotted off with me. Robert says
the weight on the shoulders is simply crushing,
and yet four men (two and two by turns), whose
height may average five feet four inches, and
whose arms and legs are certainly not half the
size of an ordinary Englishman's, will carry me
up and down the most tremendous hillsides at
about four miles an hour. Their strength and
endurance are really marvellous, and they are
such light-hearted cheerful creatures, always
keeping enough breath for a chat, or to clamber
up an extra rock to get me some ferns or flowers.

As we were going along we were startled by
a scramble and rustle above us, and then saw a
big Langour monkey take a flying leap across
the path into the trees below, followed by a troop
of several more. They are very large grey
monkeys about as big as deerhounds, with immensely long tails and with grey whiskers round
their faces. A baby Langour could never look
young—one could not associate youth with these
venerable whiskers. It was wonderful to see
them disappear down the 'khud,' swinging and

leaping from tree to tree with extraordinary ease and swiftness.

Oct. 14.—A most ludicrous letter this morning from a native official at Meerut, who has been to see how things are going on at our house, and thus reports : ' The Fittun (phaeton) is ready and admitted in the Bungalow, and Brown coach (brougham) is nearly to be prepare. The Hens are at usual time, and also Horses in former case. The Cat with her Infant is well. Weekly I am going to Bungalow and ever pray and all thing as usual.'

I am glad the cat and her infant are well!

Oct. 16.—It is a funny sight to a new-comer on going to church to see the crowds of dandies ranged outside, looking like miniature canoes that have been beached. If the congregation consist of 200 women and 100 men, that means 200 dandies, which, with an average of three coolies to each, gives 600 attendant coolies, besides 100 ponies and 100 syces. So you can fancy the crowd outside the church. An Indian crowd, however, is never noisy or rough, and somehow or other everyone finds his pony or dandy without any trouble.

Yesterday we rode to the cemetery. It is built, like everything else, on the side of a precipitous hill, and is all in steep terraces, sometimes only wide enough to contain a single row of graves. It looks very lonely and peaceful.

Oct. 17.—As we were out on the western hills we stopped to speak to a woman who was tending cattle. She was a Thibetan, and, though clothed in very filthy-looking rags and with a dirty blanket over her head, she had several quaint and handsome ornaments round her neck. I called her to me, and began asking the value of them, which she knew to a nicety—so much for the silver, so much the workmanship. She had on three or four strings of large beads, alternate coral and turquoises, the latter as big as hazel-nuts, but of a greenish hue with black flaws in them, very much like thrushes' eggs. One of her necklets was of coral beads and silver tags, and took my fancy greatly. I

wished to buy it, and we began bargaining.
While we were talking, two small sons of hers
crept up to my dandy, which was on the ground,
and inspected me with deep wonder and curiosity.
At last the eldest boy furtively stretched out his
hand and touched the fur on my jacket, much
as one might touch a sleeping snake; the little
one was rather awestruck at his brother's boldness, but, as if fascinated by the fur, crept nearer
and nearer, and suddenly darted out his hand
to touch it, drawing down his mother's anger
on him for his rudeness.

The natural good manners of these natives
are striking, their perfect self-possession and
absence of all shyness, and their politeness.

The woman finally consented to part with
her necklace for a mere trifle over its actual
worth, and her brother, a hideous Thibetan with
only one eye, returned home with us to receive
the money. I have unstrung the necklace and
given the silver to be purified with fire, and
have washed the coral in boiling water. These
hill people wear their ornaments day and night

for years, and are anything but clean in their persons.

Oct. 18.—This morning we went to the bazaar to try and find some brooch to match the necklace, but without any success. Suddenly who should appear but our Thibetan friend, who came up smiling, and said she had many other ornaments at the Treasurer's if we would like to see them. So we waited till she returned, bringing a cloth cap of many colours, quite covered with turquoises and silver ornaments. These hill people invest all their savings in jewellery, which is at any time convertible into money again with little or no loss, as the silver or gold was paid for by weight and will always be worth the same, and the value of the workmanship is well known, being from $1\frac{1}{2}d.$ to $3d.$ in the shilling for silver.

How different this is from English jewellery, the intrinsic value of which bears sometimes a scarcely appreciable proportion to the price charged for the ornament. No wonder the English goldsmiths require protective duties.

Oct. 20.—We went yesterday to the Kempti
Falls, six miles off, and a descent most of
the way. The party consisted of our two
selves. The day was lovely, and during the
night snow had fallen on a distant mountain
range, making its jagged peaks dazzling white in
the sunshine.

When we got within sight of the Falls we
stopped in the dense shadow of a broad-leaved
tree, and there ate our luncheon, while an old
Rájpút from a village near by brought us water
from a spring. We had a long talk with him,
and found that his village belongs to the Tíri
Rája. Its yearly rental is assessed at fourteen
rupees, but the old man added that, what with
forced labour and taxes on cattle and firewood, it
came to about forty.

The view from above the Falls is very beautiful. The only visible sign of civilization is
the telegraph-wire between Landour and Simla.
That is a never-ending marvel to me. You see
this one slender wire bridging over the most
precipitous valleys, taking a leap of 500 yards

from one hill to the next, and suspended 1,000 feet in the air, and you know that at that moment some message 'big with fate' may be flying along it.

Oct. 21.—The Landour bazaar is an amusing place to stroll through. The shops are very much like cow-stalls, about eight feet square, the flooring raised some two feet or more above the road, and the front entirely open to the street. The street is very narrow, so that a pony kicking or a dandy turning round can cause a block. It is the only road between Mussoorie and Landour, and is' often thronged with people.

The goldsmiths and cobblers and tailors all sit cross-legged amongst their goods, pursuing their work with the greatest composure, chatting with the passers-by, or ready at any time to make a bargain with a customer. Their time does not seem to be very precious. They pay little house-rent, sink no capital in a stock of goods, and can afford to take life easily.

They all have their names in English over

their shops, and some are very comical.
'*Juggoo*, Eggsman,' '*Kási Náth*, Dressmaker of
Gents and Ladies,' '*Jaláloodeen*, Moderate Price
Shop,' '*Rám Láll*, Shopkeeper,' '*Yusuf Moham-
mud*, Sweeties and Jams.'

Oct. 24.—We returned yesterday evening
from an expedition to Lakwâr, a dâk bungalow
about fifteen miles from here on the road to
Chakráta. We started the day before, in the
morning, Robert and I riding, but with my
dandy in attendance as well, as it rests me to go
down the hills in it. Besides this we had coolies
to carry our bundles of bedding, some eatables,
and a few odds and ends.

The road is generally eight or ten feet wide,
but sometimes only three or four, with bits of
loose rock lying about. The khuds are very
steep, sometimes a sheer descent of 1,500 feet
into the valley, where a beautiful mountain
stream, the Aglár, foams and dashes along in
its haste to join the great Jumna.

The last two miles down to the Jumna are
very beautiful, the hillside covered with a thick

jungle of trees and underwood, the foliage varied and beautiful, and many flowering shrubs and creepers. One bell-shaped creeper—some clematis, I think—has a powerful scent like the magnolia. Another we call the hyacinth-shrub (*Hamiltonia suaveolens*), as its flower smells exactly like a double-hyacinth in a warm room.

We crossed the Jumna on a suspension-bridge ; the river bed there is not more than 150 feet wide, and at this season the stream is only half that width. The water is a cool clear green, deep and very rapid, dashing into sheets of foam where it meets a rock. Its course is very winding, not to say wriggling. The wonder is that it finds its way at all among such mountains! Occasionally a huge landslip occurs, blocking up its course altogether. What a rage it must get in before it manages to cut its way through again !

From the Jumna there is a steep ascent of three miles along bare and precipitous khuds, and here we met some cows with their calves, which gave me a fright. They passed us in a skittish way, which is not pleasant when you are riding on a mantel-shelf; but still they had gone by, and were all right as I thought, when they caught sight of Robert's syce, who was wearing an old red uniform, and, taking fright at this apparition, they turned suddenly round, charged up the hill again, knocking their driver head over heels as they did so, hustled past us, and then disappeared down a spur of the hill. I was truly thankful to see the last tail vanish, for panic-stricken cattle are very awkward things on a mountain road. Their unfortunate driver had hurt his back in his fall, but he might easily have broken his neck instead. I pitied him, poor man, having to go down that steep hillside after his beasts.

Lakwâr is a pretty village, rather like a Swiss one, the houses being built with immense projecting caves, and great rough slabs of slate for a roof. The upper storey is all of wood, with carved balconies, and projects far beyond the lower one.

The dâk bungalow is close to the village. It has only two rooms, both of which were

occupied by travellers. Luckily for us, Mr. Ross, the Superintendent of the Doon, had his tent pitched there, of which we took possession in his absence. It was of course a hill tent, twelve feet square, which does not leave much room after two beds are put in. However, we were most fortunate to get it at all, and after dinner lay down (having no chairs), and read luxuriously as long as our two candles lasted.

We slept soundly, but were waked at day-break by the chattering of the servants outside, whom we could not contrive to silence.

CHAPTER XII.

MEERUT AGAIN—LOVE OF HOME FADES AT 80°—85 LBS. OF
    BAGGAGE—HERBERT ROBERTS'S HAND BILLIARDS—TROOPS
    CROSSED FRONTIER—FEVER RAGING—NATIVE RENDER-
    ING OF ENGLISH NAMES—ANTIPATHY TO CATS—TAME-
    NESS OF ANIMALS IN INDIA—SUFFERINGS OF CAMP-
    FOLLOWERS IN CÁBUL.

Meerut, Oct. 29.—Here we are once more, and
inclined to agree with the sentiment that there
is no place like home, *up to about 85°*! Love of
home fades at that degree, and entirely dies out
at 10° higher.

Just now the weather is really beautiful,
ranging from 68° to 80° indoors during the
twenty-four hours, and it is quite possible to
drive out in the middle of the day in a carriage
with a hood to it.

Most of the troops have gone to the front,
and we have come back to a deserted station.

Every second bungalow is empty, and the very walls and verandahs have a deserted look that I cannot account for.   Patches where the plaster has fallen off, but which one never noticed before, now show in a most obtrusive manner.   Pillars which must long have been cracked, but which always have looked cheerful enough before, now look wrecked and ruined.   The air of desolation is curious.

Opinions are very various about the coming war and its results.   The station pessimist is loud in proclaiming his cheerful belief that another six months will see us, or the remnant that may be left of us, flying for our lives to the seaports.

Many think it madness to engage in this war.   Many think it would be sheer folly and inanity *not* to engage in it.   So anyone may think what he likes and be sure of not being alone in his opinion.

An officer has just been here to wish us good-bye before starting for the frontier.   He was telling me of his struggles to reduce his

' necessaries ' to the regulation 80 lbs. of baggage allowed. He first apportioned a certain weight to bedding, and, having made a sack, proceeded to put in what blankets and things he thought necessary for passing his nights out—in the snow very probably. This done, he weighed it—to find it, alas! nearly twice what he expected. So he had regretfully to pull out what he thought could best be spared, and then weigh again, but without a much better result. He finally came to the conclusion that *nothing* would go for the regulation weight, and that he had better put as much on his body as he could, after the fashion of the Chinese palanquin-bearers. When they begin to carry you, they look to be enormous men, nearly as broad as they are high. After a mile or so they stop and take off a coat. The second mile brings off a second coat, until they have dwindled into mere frames of men, human clothes-pegs!

Nov. 1.—Last night we had some people to dinner, and afterwards we all adjourned to the Club to see Herbert Roberts, the Champion

Hand-stroke Billiard-player, who is making the tour of India this cold season. He gives 350 in 600 to any amateur. He himself does not use a cue, and has the privilege of playing his own ball each time from any place he chooses. The ball seems absolutely alive in his hand. It did the most impossible things, going straight for some way and then turning sharp round a corner just where it was wanted. One thing made every one laugh. Roberts had holed the red, and, taking it out, threw it up the table to the marker to spot. The marker (a native) put out his hand to stop it, when it suddenly recoiled, like a live thing, without his touching it, and ran swiftly back down the table. The marker's face was worth seeing.

Roberts made no break that night over 100, though he has made breaks, I believe, of 1,500 and 1,700. He won the game, however, easily, and then gave an exhibition of trick strokes. He placed three dinner-plates on the table and set a billiard-ball spinning in each. This done, he emptied the fifteen pyramid balls out of their wicker bottle, and then, taking a cue, shot one ball after another back into its mouth as it lay on the table, each ball taking the jump with absolute precision and with great force and rapidity. All this was done while the three balls were spinning in the plates. It was a curious and amusing exhibition.

Nov. 10.—We are all waiting anxiously for the 20th, on which day, if the Amír's answer has not arrived or is unsatisfactory, war is to be declared. The spirit of the great native chiefs seems most loyal and friendly. The Begum of Bhopál, the Nizam. Kashmir, and most of the Punjáb chiefs have offered us troops and help. Scindia and Holkar alone have not yet shown their hands ; a suggestion was made for forcing them by asking them to lend us their transport animals, which would effectually 'draw their teeth,' as it would leave them an army indeed, but with no means of moving it. No doubt they are waiting to see how events shape themselves, and intend to act accordingly. If we meet with success in Cábul, they will be

our humble and devoted servants ; if we meet
with reverses—we shall see.

Nov. 14.—Yesterday we had our second
garden party, but many people were absent,
having gone to see the 39th Native Infantry
start for the front. As soon as our last guest's
departure set us free, we too drove to the railway station in the hope of being in time to wish
them good-bye, but we only arrived in time to
see the train steaming out of the station.

Every preparation is being made for war in
earnest. Women and children have been sent
away from Peshawur, and no officers' wives are
allowed to go further west than Rawul Pindi.
Many officers would allow no women to stay
further west than this is.

Nov. 22.—A private telegram last night to
say ' Troops crossed frontier to-day,' so it is to
be war. We shall not hear much, for it is said
the press has been gagged, and military officers
forbidden to send any information. It is very
tantalizing to us here, but we quite admit the
wisdom of it, for what we heard others might

hear. Many military men think the press has become a most mischievous nuisance in war time, and would gladly see Correspondents treated as spies. But what would Londoners do? Are not telegrams hot from the seat of war among the daily necessaries of their lives?

Wednesday evening there was a dance, and we made up a party to go. We could not but think of the ball at Brussels on the eve of Waterloo. I do not think I could have gone to that dance if Robert had been at the front, and perhaps to storm the Khyber Pass next day! However, people feel things differently, and many women were there whose husbands are with the army.

Nov. 24.—Alas for my poor little cat!

> Ding dong bell,
> Pussy's in the well!
> Who put her in ?

Nobody knows, but the bhisti pulled her out, and an open verdict of 'Found drowned' has been returned. Poor little cat, it was a tragical end. Her mother bears her infant's loss philosophically, and even the puppy keeps up his spirits and appetite quite undiminished.

A very meagre telegram to say that our troops advanced on Ali Musjid and occupied the fort, which had been evacuated.

Yesterday I had a present from a native banker at Simla of some delicious hill honey. It is the first Indian honey I ever tasted, and is clear and delicate-flavoured, much like Narbonne honey.

Nov. 25.—There is a great deal of fever about of a very bad kind. It is raging in the District, and at Delhi the people are dying at the rate of 120 a day, a death-rate that would exterminate the population in less than five years. A report has been received from Shádera that 5,000 persons are ill with fever, and this out of a population of 7,000.

The Jumna floods were very widespread this year, and the malaria they left after subsiding is the cause of this frightful mortality.

The thermometer now indoors ranges from 72° to 60°; but the odd thing is how cold we feel this to be. We sleep under three blankets, sit round a fire every evening, wear ulsters out driving, and flannel from head to foot.

Our troops will suffer terribly from cold this winter. Mrs. A—— heard this week from her husband, who is at Rawul Pindi, and who describes the cold in tents as most severe. He says he has to sleep in his thickest tweed suit and ulster, and as many blankets as he can get. It is no wonder that a good many of the native doolie-bearers and others have deserted. I believe they are very insufficiently clothed, poor fellows.

Mr. Melville has returned, so Robert is now Collector again, and we shall shortly be going into camp.

Ever since our return from the hills there has been quite an epidemic of calling; every morning several sets of callers, till the table is covered with a snowstorm of cards. Owing to the inability of native servants for pronouncing English names, you always send in cards when calling, and if the lady is at home you receive a 'salaam.'

The native rendering of Wordsworth is *Wadswad*, of Alexander *Sikunder*, of Smith *Ischmitt*. Under these names you cannot always recognise your friends.

Dec. 2.—Colonel E—— has just been calling here. Whilst he was talking to me I saw the door pushed open and my old cat come in. Now I knew that Colonel E—— has an antipathy to cats, and I hardly knew what I had better do, but as he was sitting with his back to the door I hoped he would not observe her. She came along behind him, and went out at the verandah door, but just as she was passing he turned round, grasped the arms of his chair, and seemed to become quite rigid. I jumped up and shut the doors, and he just escaped having a fit. He says the antipathy is inherited from his mother, who would faint dead if a cat passed near her. He has done all he could to overcome it, by having a kitten and trying to accustom himself to it, but the effort used so to exhaust him that doctors forbade his continuing it. He says that more than once he has been found in a fit, and that he has no power of keeping a cat away. He has tried to hit them with a stick, but his arm feels paralysed when he tries, and he can neither hit them nor throw anything at them. He says he is certain he could not hit one if he fired at it.

This is the second case I have personally known of this extraordinary antipathy to cats. It is most strange.

The first dish of early peas to-day. Salads and all vegetables are now beginning to come in.

Camp, Dec. 9.—Once more we find ourselves in tents, for probably our last season, as Robert is sure to be made a judge before next winter, and judges do not go out into camp.

It is sometimes inconvenient being forty miles from one's butcher and baker. Our dâk-runners failed to turn up yesterday, so we have had no bread for two days, and have had to eat the chupatties of the country, thin unleavened cakes of flour and water. Some people profess to like them. They seem to me to be food for dogs,—as turnips are for sheep, and hard-boiled eggs for canaries !

On Thursday we dined at the General's, and he told me that just before dinner he had received a telegram ordering him to go at once to take the command at Rawul Pindi. He said his wife did not know of it, and begged me not to mention it. What a *bouleversement* of all their plans ! It is quite uncertain how long he may be away, and will probably depend on the duration of the Cábul campaign.

Dec. 19.—A young civilian lately come to India told me the other day that what had struck him most on his arrival had been the tameness of the wild birds and beasts (excepting of course *game* which is accustomed to being hunted). It certainly is striking, and shows a radical difference in the Asiatic and European character. English boys instinctively catch or pursue—or I fear hurt and plague—any live thing they see, with a few arbitrary exceptions in the shape of pets. Hindustani boys would never dream of throwing a stone at a bird or beast, or shouting at them, or in any way annoying them except in self-defence. And the result of this is seen in the impudence of the crows and monkeys, the impertinence of the sparrows—who while you are at dinner will hop about, picking up crumbs without any fear of the servants—the boldness of the village dogs, in spite of occasional tent-pegs thrown at them when they have carried off some one's chupatties—and the general confidence and tameness of the squirrels and small birds.

Even the vultures only hop lazily out of the way when any one passes. In England what a life they would lead!

Dec. 22.—It is painful to hear of the sufferings of the camp-followers with our army in Cábul. The cold there is bitter. Our cold here, which we feel so keenly, is summer weather compared with it, and the miserable kahárs (carriers of baggage and of litters for invalids) have been sent to face this cold with no shelter at night, and with no warm clothing but *one blanket* generously provided by Government. It is simple murder. And you must remember that many and many of the poor creatures have

been forced away from their homes entirely
against their will. A staff officer writing says :
' It is no exaggeration to say that the line of our
march has been marked by the skeletons of the
kahárs who have died of exposure and cold,
fallen out of the ranks, and been torn to pieces
by vultures and wild beasts. The suffering has
been cruel.'

Vessels full of water *inside* the tents are
frozen into a solid lump of ice, and these helpless miserable natives are sent to such a
climate to pass their nights in the open *with
one blanket*. It makes one's heart ache for
them ; but I fear it is a case in which private
charity cannot interfere. It is essentially a
matter for the Government, and the ways of
Government are tardy and inscrutable.

We are getting up a fund at Meerut to
supply materials for a Working Bee to make
warm clothing to send to the soldiers, just for
Christmas presents. The workers are the
women of the regiments which have gone to the
front.

In two days more the Christmas holidays begin, and we mean to make a rush into Rájputána and see what we can in the few days allowed us. Perhaps we may even go to Agra.

CHAPTER XIII.

JAIN TEMPLE AT DELHI—ULWAR—A SUBLIME COACH-HOUSE—
LIBRARY AND ARMOURY—JAIPÚR—SCHOOL OF ART—
PUBLIC GARDENS—AMBÊR—AJMEER—A CAVALRY SAINT—
TÁRA GURH—JAIN-MAHOMMEDAN TEMPLE—A BIG COOK-
ING-POT.

Ulwar, Christmas Day, 1878.—We left the
camp at two o'clock yesterday, going by rail to
Delhi. As we had some hours to wait there we
drove about the city, an ever-fresh pleasure to
me. We went to see a Jain temple, to which we
had to walk some little way through a narrow
lane of high houses. We had once to take
refuge under a carved wooden gateway while some
panic-stricken cows rushed by ; the instant they
saw us they turned tail and fled helter-skelter.
They saw we were not ' mild Hindus,' and feared
us accordingly. It was the more tiresome as I
wanted to examine some picturesque necklets

they were wearing, made of cowries sewn in fanciful patterns on red cloth. However, they rushed by in such a way that no one could catch them.

The Jain temple has a fine frontage of carved stone, carved so profusely in such delicate airy tracery that it is difficult to believe it is stone. We went up a flight of steps and came to a courtyard surrounded by what we call Moorish arches, with colonnades having groined roofs, every inch of which was painted elaborately with graceful arabesques, the effect being rich and soft in the extreme.

On one side of the courtyard is the temple proper, on a raised daïs four feet high. The building and decorations are exquisite; the shafts of all the arches are of polished white marble inlaid with flowing flowery patterns in coloured marbles. The walls and ceiling and every available inch are painted richly, the prevailing colours being blue and gold, but all so artistically blended that the eye only takes in the general effect, which is something like that of a Cashmere shawl.

In the centre, under the dome, is a very beautiful shrine for the idol, who is sitting serenely at a height of ten feet or so under a fine baldachino of white inlaid marble. If the whole could be transported to Italy, and a statue of the Virgin substituted for the idol, its beauty would be raved about. A sparrow was perched familiarly on the shrine, and gave us some little friendly chirps to show he did not object to our presence.

The attendant priest told us the temple had cost 30,000*l.* seventy years ago, when labour was even cheaper than it is now. The Jains are a sect of Hindus dating from very ancient times, but quite modern Dissenters by the side of the Buddhists.

We left Delhi at ten o'clock, travelling all night, and arrived here at seven this morning in the cold grey dawn. This Rájputána railway is not a delight. The gauge is very narrow, and the jolting surprising. At starting the sensation is as if the engine reared, and then gave two or three plunges before fairly settling down.

After that you merely feel as if the train were travelling along toothed rails, hop, hop, hop. Then the engine, during a stoppage, would relieve itself by bellowing in a way I never heard a civilized engine do, waking me from the only snatch of sleep I got.

After having some breakfast at the dâk bungalow, we drove out in a carriage the Residency Surgeon had sent us to see the city of Ulwar. It is prettily situated, with a background of rocky hills close to it, crowned by a long line of fortifications. The city wall is very imposing, with great bastions and enormous gates studded with long spikes, on which hundreds of pigeons roost at night, and by the appearance of the gates have done so for many generations.

The town is too much modified by English taste and style to be very interesting, though the long line of bazaar is picturesque and notably clean. We went to see the Rája's coach-house, where he has about forty vehicles of various descriptions, one dating from Lord Lake's time, when carriages must have been scarce. The whole place was kept so preternaturally clean and neat that it evidently inspires the native servants with awe, for they all left their shoes at the entrance ! Fancy the sublimity of a coach-house that could constrain you to take off your hat !

We also visited the Rája's horses, I cannot say *stables*, as they are all picketted out in a large enclosure. He is said to have 500 horses, but some are at his other residences. The horses did not attract me much, excepting one mite of a pony that we measured, and found to be thirty-four inches high.

The palace itself is very fine, all built of stone, with a façade several hundred feet in length, rich with deep balconies and oriel win- dows, supported on stone carved brackets as delicate as point-lace—a singularly beautiful building. And what do you think this façade overlooks ? A huge, untidy, squalid enclosure, with 100 horses picketted in the centre, and mud huts and thatched sheds in every stage of

disrepair all round.   This is true native fashion,
wholly uncorrupted by English habits.

Inside there is a huge hall of audience,
gorgeously carpetted, and adjoining it is a small
narrow room decorated from floor to roof entirely
in coloured glass mosaic, most splendid in its
colour and glitter. We were told it employed
a large number of workmen for fifteen years.
From the carved marble arches of this little
room you look out on a most theatrical scene ;
a large piece of artificial water, with long flights
of steps leading down to it the whole way round,
broken only by bastions running out into the
water, and each having on it a slender white
marble kiosk, dazzling white in the sun.   Rising
immediately behind it are the jagged red rocks,
with the fort cutting the sky line.   I could be
very fond of that cool glass room with its lovely
outlook.

There are extensive ranges of zenana apartments, which you can tell by the jealously-
guarded balconies—all one mass of stone lacework, with never an opening big enough for a

pigeon to pass through. Safe behind these screens the ladies can look on at all that goes on in the courtyard of the durbar hall.

The Rája has a very valuable library, collected principally by his grandfather. I was much interested in an exquisitely illuminated copy of the 'Gulistán,' for which 5,000*l*. was paid! It is a marvel of patience, delicacy, and fancy, and would compare well with any European illuminations, though totally different in character. Much of it is pen work. I spent a long time examining its beauties. It is a very different library from another I remember seeing, belonging to a native prince in Oudh, in which the books had chiefly been selected, like the men in Frederick the Great's body-guard, *for their size*. Tall encyclopædias and ponderous histories, and all such other books as ' no gentleman's library should be without '—little to read, but much to look at—and here and there three little books standing one atop of the other to make up the required height.

Then the armoury, too, is interesting. Swords

there are of fabulous value, some of which we inspected narrowly ; but I own to sharing King James's dislike to a naked blade. I was glad when they were done with, and we passed on to curious old flint-lock guns, with finely-chased and inlaid barrels, and armour of all kinds.

One helmet was quite different from any I ever saw, and looked as if it had belonged to a Viking. It had branching steel weapons on it, most wild and weird-looking.

We also went to see another of the Rája's palaces, two miles off, where the grounds are really well laid out in Italian fashion. We saw a quantity of lynxes, kept for hunting hares, and a fine cheetah or leopard ; he seemed as gentle and tame as a dog, and was sitting in one of the streets, only tied to a post. He had a leathern hood thrown back on his forehead, just as old people put up their spectacles when they don't want them. They say he is obliged to have the hood drawn over his eyes if any goats are passing, or he would spring on one.

Jaipúr, Dec. 26.—We ate our Christmas

dinner at the Ulwar dák bungalow, faring sumptuously on what provisions we in our fore-sight had brought with us, eked out with some mutton (called sheep that morning), which made us some broth.

At nine o'clock we got into the train, and arrived here this morning at eight, behind our time, having crawled along for some while at five miles an hour.

Colonel Beynon, the Political Agent here, very kindly pressed us to be his guests during our stay, but we prefer the independence of hotels or dâk bungalows. It sometimes suits us to go to bed just when other people would be going to dinner.

Jaipúr is a thoroughly native city, but ut-terly different from most others. It is built in blocks, with streets at right angles to each other, the widest 110 feet wide, the next 55 feet, and the next half as narrow again. The whole city is surrounded by a high wall built of red stone cut into vandykes at the top, and having at a distance the appearance of a huge red paling.

There is a School of Art, supported entirely by the Rája, and intended to improve native art. We went all over it and saw the different manufactures in progress—embroidering, inlaying, stone-carving, engraving on brass, electroplating, and so on. It was interesting, but I myself think it will do more to debase and destroy true native art than anything. Instead of merely encouraging and developing native design and colouring, it attempts in many instances to substitute European ideas and patterns. Its result is already seen in the many ugly and uninteresting copies of European designs, and, if continued in, it must inevitably destroy the characteristic style which is the great charm of Indian work.

We made an expedition on foot—the street being too narrow for a carriage—to find out the native workers in marble. Shops they have none, but we followed our guide into a little courtyard, where marble in blocks and slabs, and half-hewn statues of idols, lay in confusion everywhere. Here we sat down, and the stone-carver brought us quite a large selection of specimens. A large crowd of people collected round us, immensely interested in our proceedings. We finally gave orders for a tripod of elephants, supporting a bowl for flowers, all in the white Jaipúr marble. It is something like alabaster, and will contrast well with flowers and foliage.

The palace here is an enormous one, a perfect town in itself, but with nothing striking or unique that I noticed except its size. We went up to the top of its highest building, about 150 feet, which you ascend by a series of gradients as you do the campanile of St. Mark's. From the top you get a wide view of the whole city and the country beyond, and I can fancy the Rája looking with pride on his fair kingdom. The present man is fifty, and has seven wives, but no children. So much we gleaned from the servants ; but they evidently disliked being questioned, and when I asked in which part of the palace the Ránis' apartments were, they said, looking eastward, ' They are in this direction, but we cannot point them out.' Such etiquette is more than Spanish in its respectfulness!

There are very large public gardens too, kept up at an immense expense, which almost grieves one when one thinks how hard up the people are. Gram is selling at 12 srs. and wheat at 10 srs. to the rupee, quite famine prices.

In the gardens are kept tigers, panthers, deer of many kinds, and some large and well-stocked aviaries. We were amused to see numbers of rats scuttling about the owls' place, with a great horned owl benevolently watching them. The squirrels and sparrows also find they can pass through the wire netting, and, grain being dear, they go in and eat sociably at Government expense.

The tigers are better housed here than at Ulwar, where it made me miserable to see them. They were in cold dark cages paved with flagstones, sluiced with water by way of cleaning them, and having no kind of drainage. The poor beasts all had terrible raw places on their feet, and must really suffer cruelly. We saw two lovely panther cubs a month old cuddling up to their father for warmth, and were told their mother died on Tuesday of cold.

Jaipúr, Dec. 27.—To-day we have been to see Ambêr, the ancient capital. We drove the first few miles, passing numberless beautiful native residences peeping out of groves and gardens, now nearly all deserted since the seat of Government has been changed.

About two miles before reaching Ambêr the road rises pretty steeply, and, a hill being unknown in these parts of India, it is considered quite out of the question for a carriage to go either up or down such a perilous place! So there was an elephant waiting there for us. As we went leisurely along we saw quantities of peafowl as tame as chickens, and great Langour monkeys skipping about in the trees.

The Ambêr Palace is on an abrupt hill, and looks very imposing with its long irregular massive line. It is very beautiful, and must have cost the Rája many a pang to desert.

The marble shafts and arches, and carved marble panels and lacework screens, are exquisitely beautiful. I spent some time in trying to sketch some of the bewilderingly intricate designs of a screen, and a spray of inlaid-work, but grew impatient over my own incompetency. An artist might live there for a month, and find full occupation in copying the arabesques and other designs so lavishly scattered everywhere. It makes one sad to see it deserted.

As we passed through Jaipúr on our way back it was the busiest time of the day, between four and five o'clock, and the bazaar was crowded. This place reminds me in much of Italy. The streets are really noble, and the great open squares as fine as any European ones. The houses are not as high as in Europe, but far more picturesque, with a great deal of colour about them, and beautifully broken in outline by oriel windows and projecting upper storeys, all supported on carved stone brackets, with long lines of pierced screens in red stone or white marble, one more delicate and beautiful

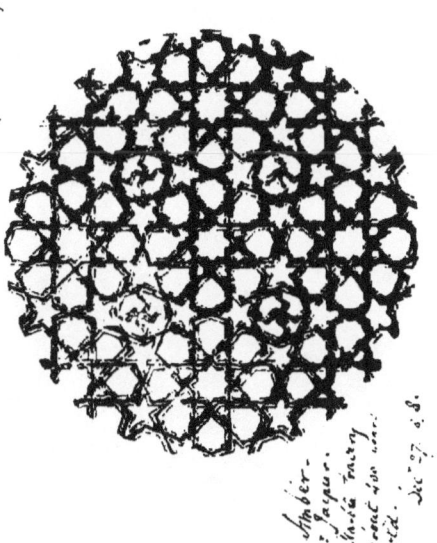

than the other ; and here and there gateways with the graceful slender-shafted kiosks you see everywhere.

There is one campanile with a marble cupola at top, very Italian in effect. But the bazaar and the awnings, and the humped white bullocks, and the white or gay colouring of the crowds, and the elephants and camels—all these belong only to India, and make the scene more brilliant and picturesque than anything Western could be. It is a never-ending pleasure to me.

Jaipúr is quite a model town in many ways. It is absolutely lighted with gas! and the lamp-posts are as straight and the glasses as clean as if it were Paris. Water, too, is pumped up by machinery into a large reservoir, and thence supplied to the whole town. There are posts all along the streets, with taps to them, and often a little thatched roof over them, where the people fill their brass pots and waterskins in the utmost comfort. It must be the greatest luxury to them, and they must heartily bless their Rája.

I am extremely glad to have seen a place

still under native rule, but I cannot think Jaipúr
can be taken as a fair specimen of one. If it
were, the cities in our territory would compare
badly with it.

Dec. 29.—We left Jaipúr yesterday for
Ajmeer. Our train was to leave at eight o'clock,
so we got up in due time by candlelight. At
the station we found Colonel Beynon come to
meet some friends he expected, but the Rájputána line takes things easily, and we heard from
the station-master that he had just had a telegram
saying the train was late and could not be in for
another two hours !

This being certain, we started off to drive to
the Ghaut, some miles from Jaipúr. It was a
drive well worth taking, extremely pretty and
uncommon; down a fairly steep hill, with picturesque minarets and cupolas on either side,
embowered in trees, and backed by high rocky
hills. I almost forgot it was India.

We got back just as our train came in, and
finally got off at 10.15. It takes six hours to
get to Ajmeer, and the road lies through dreary

scenery. A huge wild plain, sandy and barren, with no growing thing but tussocks of high grass and ugly clumps of dusty cactus, with here and there some stunted palm-trees. In the distance low reddish hills, all looking hot and desolate. As you get near Ajmeer the hills close in, and at last the train takes a great curve round a spur of rock, and you see the city before you, nestling at the very foot of the hills. There is a pretty lake made by a great dam run across the valley in the old days of Mahommedan rule.

This morning we got a splendid.view of the whole city and surrounding country from the Tára Gurh, the ancient fortress on the hill above the town. We rose early and started soon after sunrise, Robert on a pony and I in a chair called here a tánján, carried by eight men. We passed through the city gate, which is studded thickly with horse-shoes. We were told that in olden days, when any one presented a horse to the saint whose tomb is at Tára Gurh, a shoe was nailed on to the gate in commemoration. To judge by the shoes, the saint must have had a large force of cavalry.

The way to the fort lies up a valley through extensive ruins, where once an ancient town has been. The road ascends for a mile or two, and then, leaving the valley, climbs by sharp zigzags and steep gradients up a precipitous rocky hill which is crowned by the old fort. It is now quite a ruin, but grand in its decay. It is over 1,000 years old, and must have been absolutely impregnable before the invention of heavy artillery.

There is a huge tank in it which is filled by the rains, and would last the garrison till the next rainy season; so they would not have to surrender from thirst.

In the fort is the mausoleum of the horsey saint. We were told that from the top we should get a splendid view, so we went up. Two of the steps are quite three feet high, others a foot or more, and the last turn, besides being very narrow, has no parapet on the outer side. It was not altogether pleasant, and in coming

down I came like a crab, sideways and backwards. The view is very extensive, but not
beautiful at all ; merely a bird's-eye view of
what we saw from the train. You look almost
straight down on the white city, and you see
the ruins of the wonderful wall of giant blocks
running straight down the steepest scarp of the
hill from the fort to the valley.

Inside the fort are modern barracks and
hospitals for our soldiers; white and ugly after
the pattern of the Public Works Department for
ever. The fort has stood while the Hindu and
Mahommedan dynasties have risen and passed
away, and now stands while the Christian rules
in the land. It makes one wonder what other
changes it is destined to see.

On our way down we went to see another
curious and glorious monument of the changes
brought about by time ; an old Hindu temple,
afterwards turned by the Mussulman conquerors
into a mosque. Fortunately they did not destroy the original building, which is still there
in almost perfect repair, with most of the domes

and carved stone pillars as fresh and sharp in their lines as if chiselled last year instead of 1,300 or 1,400 years ago.

The Mussulmans contented themselves with smashing the idols and the stone tablets with inscriptions on them, and building a magnificent façade in front of the temple, rich beyond description with Arabic carving, and with texts from the Korán sculptured round each of the five glorious arches it consists of. The idols which the Mussulmans smashed in their zeal have lately been found while excavations were being made close by—as well as six stone tablets with their inscriptions sharp and clear. They have all been restored to their places in the temple, but the Mussulmans go there to worship as usual, and I suppose look upon the idols now as merely carved stones not in themselves offensive.

There is another famous shrine at Ajmeer; but as that saint's sanctity requires even Englishmen to take off their boots, and no button-hooks are supplied, we did not go to see that shrine. The principal curiosity there, I believe, is an enormous copper vessel—a Dêg, as it is called—which will cook eighty maunds of rice, and is only used when some charitable person volunteers to fill it for the benefit of the priests and the poor. A maund equals 80 lbs., and, at the present price of rice, the Dêg cannot be filled under a cost of 40l., as a quantity of ghee (clarified butter) has to be mixed with the rice for cooking.

We got into the train for Agra at one o'clock, and I have been writing up my journal during our stoppages. This Rájputána railway hurries no one. I have had plenty of time. We expect to reach Agra to-morrow morning at nine o'clock.

CHAPTER XIV.

AGRA—THE TÂJ—MOGUL ARRANGEMENT FOR JUDICIAL SEPARA-
TIONS—FATTEHPÚR SÍKRI—SHEIK SULÍM'S TOMB—JUMP-
ING WELL—EASTERN AND WESTERN IDEAS OF A TOMB—
AKBÁR'S TOMB—NATURAL GENTLE BREEDING OF HINDUS—
WESTERN DESTRUCTIVENESS—BROBDINGNAG MILESTONES.

Agra, Dec. 30.—I have seen the Tâj, and
have never seen anything so beautiful. I knew
it so well from photographs and sketches and
descriptions that I felt as if it would seem
familiar to me, and that I should be disappointed.

We went up the steps to the entrance gateway—in itself a grand building of red stone, very
lofty, and with a great domed roof—and when
we reached the top, and looked through the
darkness of the great arch, and saw the Tâj
gleaming in its spotless whiteness at the far end
of an avenue of shrubs and cypresses, it was so
surprisingly lovely that it brought the tears into

my eyes, just as an air of Handel's has sometimes done.

Never before has any building or any scene
had the same effect on me, and no description
can convey it to any one. It has been called a
poem in marble, a dream. But nothing can tell
you how touching and beautiful it is. Perhaps
it is its absolute spotless purity. I do not
know. But I feel as if no sight in all the world
can ever affect me as the first sight of this
did.

I wonder whether the Queen knows how
beautiful a monument her husband raised to
her! He was 'that phœnix among Eastern
princes,' the husband of one wife. He had no
other, before or after, and he lies buried by her
side. The poem was perfect.

Their tombs are under a great centre dome,
but at first I could look at nothing for listening
to the echo. Every whisper is taken up and
glorified into soft full harmony, swelling and
fading, till you seem to be listening to a distant
choir above you. One may fancy it is an angel

choir watching over the graves of such faithful lovers.

The carved marble and inlaid-work are exquisite, but only what I had expected to see. None of the details, perfect as they are, filled me in any way with the feeling of the first sight of the glorious white domes and minarets rising in their marvellous beauty against the blue sky.

We sat out in the lovely gardens of the Tâj and ate some luncheon, while the pretty grey squirrels swarmed round us and came close to our feet to pick up bits of biscuit. They particularly liked the almonds in our cake; the little rogues looked so pretty, holding it in their paws and keeping their bright eyes fixed on us.

We went all over the fort, which was Shah Jehán's palace, and where he must have often sat watching the building of his wife's tomb out on the sandy plain by the great river.

In the palace we went to see the dungeons where the Emperors used to shut up their spouses who did not please them, and saw the well where they were dropped down if they would not mend their ways. In the bathing-rooms one arrangement struck me greatly ; when the water is turned on it comes flowing over a broad shallow channel of marble some five feet up the wall, then falls to a lower level, and then falls again into the marble basin. Behind each fall there are little niches cut in the wall, each intended to hold a small lamp, so that you may see all the lights behind the sheet of falling water. The effect must be quite Arabian-Night-like!

Agra, Dec. 31.—To-day we have seen stone and marble carving which has surpassed any, not even excepting that in the Tâj, I have yet seen. We have been to Fattehpúr Síkri, a city and palace built by the great Mogul emperor Akbár, who was a contemporary of Queen Elizabeth.

It is twenty-four miles from here, so we started early and had two changes of horses. At our last stage we had a brute of a horse which came to a stand after a mile and kicked so viciously that we skipped out, and from afar watched him backing and kicking until the coachman had to let him go back to the changing place and re-harness one of the unlucky horses just taken out. If that horse can understand a moral, he will think *goodness doesn't pay*.

Fattehpúr has long been deserted except by a few villagers, and it is saddening to see the huge mounds of ruins and masses of fallen masonry and stones extending for acres and acres, with here and there a fine arch or gateway still standing among the desolation, or a massively built house still nearly perfect, standing in lonely dignity. You drive for half a mile through these ruins, and then you come to the palace, which has been kept in fair repair and is a noble building. It is all built of red stone in huge blocks, and the style throughout is Hindu, a striking memorial of Akbár's liberal-minded views, or godlessness, as his fellow-religionists called it. One of the rooms is a perfect gem, from the fabulous lavishness and beauty of its decoration. It is entirely of stone, without any wood in its construction, and the walls have exquisitely-carved panels representing hunting and forest scenes, with parrots and pheasants perching in the branches and tigers roaming through the jungles.

Sad to say, the religious zeal of the Emperor Aurangzébe in carrying out the command 'not to make graven images in the likeness of anything that is on the earth,' led him to destroy the head of every carved figure of man or bird or beast throughout the palace, so it is only headless tigers that now prowl, and headless birds that now perch in the forests.

I hope the Emperor has obtained his reward, for it was a terrible exercise of zeal.

I spent some time in sketching a few bits of ornament, one a most beautiful panel of pomegranates, which would look lovely carried out in any material. We wandered through court after court and room after room, all so massive and beautiful, and all so silent and deserted.

The gem perhaps of the whole is the tomb of a famous saint, Sulím Chisti, who died in Akbár's time. It is entirely of white marble,

and its details are more beautiful than any at
the Tâj itself. There is a centre building, a
domed room of no great size, surrounded by a
wide verandah enclosed entirely, except for the
entrance, by screens of pierced marble, so in‑
tricate and fine that they look like point-lace.
I copied the patterns of one or two, but it drives
one to despair to see the hopeless profusion of
designs, one more beautiful than another, and
most of them so intricate that it makes one's
head whirl to try and copy them.

The tomb itself is under a canopy ten or
twelve feet high, entirely covered with mother‑
o'-pearl laid on in little scales and shimmering
all over with soft rich tints. If the Tâj depended
for its beauty on its details, it would have to
give the first place to this tomb ; but, as I said
before, its details are wholly apart from and in‑
dependent of its effect ; you might sweep away
every trace of carving or inlaying that exists,
and still the Tâj would be what it is—the most
touchingly beautiful building in the world, the
spirit of Handel's 'Comfort ye' embodied in

marble. There is a sense of something beyond this world in both.

When Akbár built his Fattehpúr Palace he intended to remove the seat of government thither from Agra, and I cannot wonder at his wish. The palace at Fattehpúr is built on a high rock, something like Stirling Castle, only not on such a cramped space, and from all the balconies and gateways you have a really beautiful view of the whole country round, very different from the flat sandy plain on which Agra is built.

Just outside the palace wall is a great tank with twenty-five feet of water in it, into which men and boys jump from astonishing heights. We expressed our wish to see them, and a wonderful and rather fearful sight it is—it quite takes one's breath away. The palace wall rises sixty or seventy feet above the tank, and some men rushed up there to wait for the order to jump. I hardly liked to look at them, but when Robert called out 'Jump,' one of them leaped clean off the wall, coming hurling down, legs and arms waving, till he was close to the water, when he stiffened himself perfectly straight, and shot into the water feet foremost with a terrific shock, like a stone. He could not have gone far down, for he appeared again instantly, striking out for the steps; and then another leap, another quivering body flying through the air, another awful thud, and the second man had come down; and then in all directions you saw boys leaping in from various heights, going down like enormous frogs, the green water surging as it closed over them.

It is an extraordinary sight. They say there are only those two men who dare make the leap from the palace wall, and they only began to do so at the time of the Prince of Wales's visit in 1876. The shock must be prodigious. I wonder if it does them no harm?

I could willingly have stayed all day, and a second day, at Fattehpúr. Our time was far too short. One of the houses which belonged to Pír Bal, Akbár's Prime Minister, is turned into a dâk bungalow, and furnished sufficiently for visitors to pass the night very comfortably. It is built entirely of huge blocks of stone, and not an inch but what is carved. Victor Hugo calls it 'the tiniest of palaces, or the largest of jewel-boxes.'

We got home safely, though no thanks to that abominable horse. We twice had to jump out and then run alongside ready to jump in the moment he felt pleased to start again; and when in, we each sat with our feet on the steps ready for a jump when we thought it likely there would be a difficulty. At one time his heels were quite eight feet high; how he contrived to get his legs back again I do not know. It was too exciting to be pleasant.

Agra, Jan. 1, 1879.—We have had a quiet day, for which I was not sorry, being tired with yesterday's expedition. We went after breakfast to see the two best workers in marble inlaying, Nathu Rám and Paris Rám. There were tables and plates in every stage of finish, some only emerging from the rough block, others ready pencilled for cutting, others cut and ready for being inlaid, and others with only a few touches wanted to complete them. The workmen were all sitting on their heels in the verandahs, working leisurely and cheerily, with few and simple tools. We saw a fine table that had been ordered for Lady Howard de Walden, and another that had originally been designed as a wedding gift to the Princess of Wales, and cost 130*l*., though only two feet across.

We afterwards went to the tomb of Itmád-u-Daula, who died 250 years ago. It is on the other side of the river, and we had to cross the pontoon bridge. The tomb stands in a pretty garden, and is much on the usual model, richly ornamented in stone and marble. It is being repaired at great expense by our Government, having suffered much from long neglect and from a shock of earthquake. One of the rooms was all blackened with smoke; the natives used to stall cattle there and light fires for cooking.

This afternoon we did nothing but go to the Táj again, and sit in the gardens listening to the splash of the fountains, and enjoying the wonderful beauty before us. The sun was setting, and its soft golden light made the building look more lovely and more unreal than ever. You half expect to see it fade away as you look at it ; the outlines melt into the sky, and the shadows in the pure white marble are so faint in tone that it looks like no earthly reality. It will live in my memory while memory lasts.

How different the Eastern and Western conceptions of a tomb are ! We put our dead in gloomy lonely graves and mausoleums where everything is dismal in its solemnity. They build tombs as lovely as is possible, and have people about them, and do not seem to sever the dead from the living in the way we do. Their ordinary tombs may be seen everywhere, by the roadside, in a garden, under any tree ; not put away in lonely cemeteries, but with the tide of life flowing round them, with children playing on them and cattle grazing near, with no railings to isolate them from all around.

Gáziabad Camp, Jan. 3.—We got back to

our camp this morning at the miserable hour of
4 A.M.   However, it was dark enough to be midnight, so we went to bed immediately on reaching our tents, and I slept till. nearly noon, in
spite of the sunlight and the nearness of the
boys' school, where, to judge from the cheerful
and unceasing din, one would suppose Government's primary object was to exercise the boys'
lungs.

The rest and quiet of camp is very pleasant
after the racket and fatigue of the last week.

Yesterday we drove to Sikander, five miles
from Agra, where the great Emperor Akbár is
buried. It amazed me afresh with the surprising
magnificence of those Moguls.   The building
itself is a huge one of red stone, five storeys
high, and inlaid profusely with bold and splendid designs in white marble, and having hundreds and hundreds of yards of pierced stone-
work running round the terraces of every storey.
As Robert observed, it would cost a small fortune even to *hurdle* them all. But if the Moguls
thought anything looked well, they had as many

hundreds or thousands of yards of it as they thought would be effective, without a single thought as to what the cost might be.

The tomb stands in a large park-like enclosure with fine trees in it, and originally divided into quarters by four huge raised stone causeways, each leading to a splendid gateway. Only two of the causeways I think are now left, the others having been destroyed by the Bhurtpore Rája, and the stones carried away to build him a palace.

When one thinks of the troublous and violent times these buildings have gone through, and of the intrinsic value of their materials, it is only a matter of surprise that they should have suffered as little as they have done. It is chiefly owing to the absence in these people of the bump of destruction so strongly developed in our Western skulls. They never *wantonly* destroy or persecute or give pain. If it is to serve their purpose they are absolutely callous as to what destruction or pain they inflict ; but that is different from our Western nature, which prompts men to break windows, smash door-knockers, throw stones at birds, and set dogs at cats for no other reason than to gratify the love of wanton destruction and annoyance.

If these same Indian tombs and palaces had been in Europe for three hundred years in such times of lawless anarchy as they have passed through here, there would hardly be one stone left on another, or one piece of marble tracery unbroken. We owe much to the natural gentle breeding of these people for having done so little, and that rarely in wantonness, to hurt these noble buildings.

The top storey of Akbár's mausoleum consists of a large platform of white marble, in the centre of which is the cenotaph, of exquisitely carved marble, lying under the open sky. The entire platform is enclosed by a wall of white marble filagree of incredible variety and richness. Each side has eight or ten large divisions, and each division again has twelve panels, all different, not unlike a point-lace sampler.

The screens have occasionally a panel left

out in the centre, and through this you get a miniature view of the distant landscape, looking like a painting richly framed.

The real tomb is on the ground-floor, in a vaulted room in the very heart of the great mass. It was lighted dimly by a torch. It is quite plain, but covered by a magnificent pall of cloth of gold presented by Lord Northbrook, which, we were told, cost 500*l*.

The drive to Sikander is interesting from the many ruins along the road, and the wonderful milestones—Kós minárs—still standing, belonging to the old imperial times. They are perfect towers, very massively built, and about twenty or twenty-five feet high—milestones quite in keeping with the usual Mogul magnificence.

The country itself is sandy and dreary, covered with tamarisks, some of them very old and fine, and a shrub whose name I do not know, but which is the wickedest, spitefullest shrub in the vegetable kingdom. At a distance it looks to be an ordinary shrub, thick and bushy. You go up to it and find it is only a rudimentary shrub, for it has *no leaves*, not an attempt at one, only wicked hooked thorns that would hold like fish-hooks.   Not even a bird or a beast could find refuge in it.   One wonders why such a useless, malicious plant should exist. It seems to show that malice *pur et simple* has its use in the world.

CHAPTER XV.

IN CAMP—SÁRUS CRANES—COLONY OF SNAKE-CATCHERS—
MORTALITY OF CAMELS IN CÁBUL—MANIS CRASSICAU-
DATA—MONKEYS *v.* OLD WOMEN AT MUTTRA—INFANTI-
CIDE—POPULATION AND FOOD—PRAIRIE FIRE—CROW-
CATCHING—BACK AT MEERUT—THE BUFFS' PLATE—
JOHORE IN ENGLAND—CONFUSION OF IDEAS AS TO
OFFICIAL DIGNITIES.

Jan. 15.—We were at Gurmacktésa yesterday, and went out in the grass jungle along the
old river bank. The fickle Ganges has long ago
deserted its old bed, and now runs two miles
eastward of it. The old bank is cut up by the
rains into a labyrinth of little ravines and
gulleys, most of them with perpendicular sides
like walls. The elephant and I had a rough
time of it—I clinging on by the ropes, while he
seemed to stand on his head.

I never before saw so many of the great

crane called the Sárus as we saw to-day while marching along the low river land. We counted twenty-two in one group. They are immense birds, standing five feet high or more, and they have a wild plaintive cry that can be heard at a very great distance. There were large flocks, too, of the handsome fox-brown Brahminy ducks, who are strict monogamists, and go in pairs all the year round ; when a flock rises the birds all fly off in pairs. They are considered typical of conjugal love and faithfulness.

Jan. 21.—Still marching up the old Ganges bank. As we were going out shooting one day we passed a kind of gipsy encampment on some rising ground near the river, and on inquiring about it found it was the head-quarters of a tribe of snake-catchers. It is an odd profession for a whole tribe, is it not? Imagine educating your sons to catch snakes, and ultimately marry the daughters of other snake-catchers. It seems a narrow field. How true is the old saying that ' God giveth to some men wisdom and under-standing'—to others, the gift of catching snakes.

Their head-quarters consist of nothing but some lean-tos of grass mats, nowhere six feet high, and hardly distinguishable among the scrubby bushes. Robert sent for their chief man next day, and learnt from him all he had to tell. It appears they have been squatting here (their own term) for eighteen years, and this is known as ' The tents of Lakur Nâth.'

When we read in the Bible of the command, ' To your tents, O Israel!' visions of Aldershot rise to the English mind, and indeed I have seen a picture with the white bell tents of the most approved pattern. Israel's tents were in all probability much of the nature of this Lakur Nâth's, if indeed they existed at all, for these people frequently speak of going to their tent when they mean simply the tree under which they have spread some dry leaves for sleeping on, and where they cook and eat.

The old snake-catcher told us that there were about sixty men belonging to this tribe, but that just now he was the only person in the camp except the women and children, all the

others having gone off on two months' wander-
ing, begging as they go, and showing off their
tame snakes, of which each man has several.
He says some snakes are easily tamed, while
others take much longer. They are fed on
bread and milk, mice, frogs, and such small deer.
But they do not appear to live long, and I
should doubt their life being as merry as it is
short. It must be rather depressing to live
always coiled up in a small basket only just big
enough to hold you.

The news from Cábul is as favourable as one
could expect. We have hitherto walked over
the course with little more difficulty than was
owing to the nature of the course itself, which
has been rough enough for that of true love.

The native camp-followers and the beasts of
burden, especially the camels, have suffered
terribly. Of one convoy of 500 camels *not one*
reached Quetta alive, and from Jellálabad came
news that they were dying at the rate of two
hundred a day. It is quite terrible to think of
such sacrifice of life, and owing almost wholly to

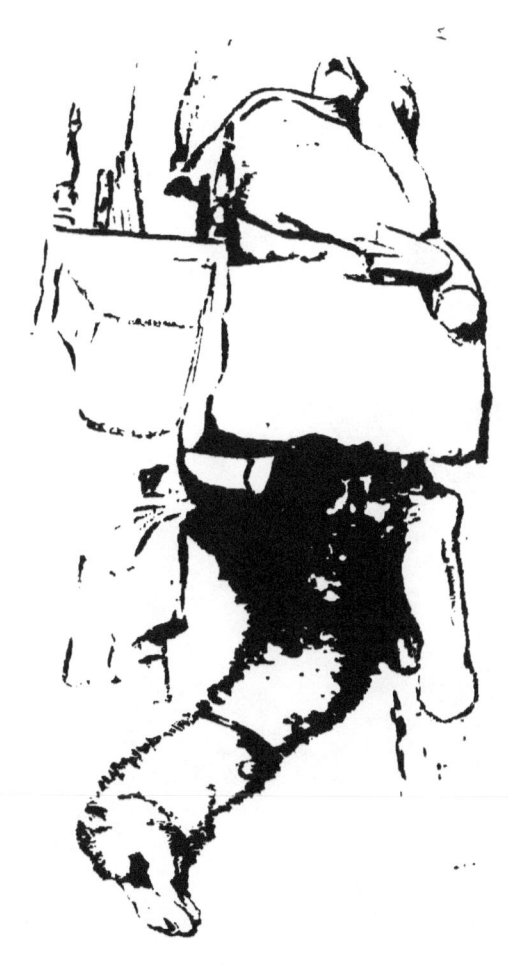

insufficient food and too hard work. Blame must of course lie somewhere, but the beautiful principle of division of labour is extended also to responsibility : and so, probably, as was the case in the 'Jackdaw of Rheims,' no one will be 'a penny the worse.'

Many of the poor patient beasts were so weak as to be quite unfit for work, and when they came to a steep descent would lose their footing and go rolling down the hillside with their loads, only lucky if they were killed outright, instead of lying with broken bones till killed piecemeal by the vultures.

Hastnapúr, Jan. 23.—Last evening out shooting we came upon three tolerably rare animals, to my great excitement—a fine shaggy hyena, a wolf, and an armadillo. Unfortunately the only one bagged was the armadillo, or, strictly speaking, *Manis crassicaudata.* He is very rare and difficult to obtain, as he lives in thick wild jungle, is extremely invisible, and rarely leaves his burrow except at night. He is exactly like a gigantic fir-cone before it begins to split.

Burnand's description of the dragon among the *dramatis personæ* of his burlesque is very applicable to him :—

> Monstrum horrendum, informe, ingens, qui—
> Regular rum 'un to look at !

When the hyena was put up Robert had only shot in his gun, so he had not even the satisfaction of sending a ball after him.

Jan. 24.—Last night we had some friends dining with us, and they were talking about Muttra and the monkeys there. Muttra is a very holy city of the Hindus, where monkeys are sacred, and allowed to do as they like. They consequently grow inconceivably bold and insolent. One gentleman was telling us how on one occasion when he was riding there he hit a monkey over the head with his hunting-whip, when in an instant fifty or sixty monkeys made a rush at him, and though he put spurs to his horse and fled, two of them managed to spring on to his horse's quarters, driving him nearly wild.

They have actually killed sundry old women by pushing them off the housetops as they sat there! It seems to me that, as they are so human and civilized in their ways, they should also bear the penalties of humanity, and be liable to being hanged for murder. But the Muttra people do not think much of old women, and a great deal of monkeys.

At Bangalore the monkeys have become a perfect pest, and a local paper says that one large monkey has taken to visiting houses in the infantry lines and laying his hands on anything that takes his fancy. The police are afraid of it, and say that the monkey must be regularly prosecuted under the Penal Code, and that they cannot arrest it.

Jan. 25.—The last few days we have had the District Superintendent of Police marching with us, who has had to inspect sundry villages near here suspected of practising female infanticide, and put therefore under special police surveillance. They have to pay themselves for the special police force, and have to report all births, and show all dead bodies of children to some police or medical authority. Their lives are in every way made a burden to them until such time as they shall see the error of their ways and consent to bring up more girls than they can provide for.

The Superintendent has been at this work now for years, and says he is perfectly certain that the practical result of our legislation is that now an equal number of boy babies are destroyed in order to balance the proportion of male and female deaths.

You cannot force parents to rear a child. You may prevent their killing it by an overdose of opium, because that can be detected and punished. But you cannot punish them when a child simply will not thrive, and after a few painful months dies ' a natural death.'

This, therefore, is another result of our efforts, that the children die a death of suffering instead of a quick and unconscious one. As to the children themselves, there can be small doubt that it is better for them to die as soon as born, than to live, to grow up and struggle, and finally die of starvation or lead a life of wickedness—and one or the other lies before these girls as long as the country is over-populated. As to the moral guilt of the parents, it cannot be great. Till we made the law against infanticide it was perhaps *nil*, for sin surely includes and signifies *consciousness of sin*, and of that they had none. It was the immemorial custom of their people, and they could not bring up more than a certain number of girls in decency.

It might perhaps be well to make England clean in this respect before interfering with these people ; and when such things as baby-farms are no longer known in Christian England, and no such things as foundling hospitals needed, then to begin to remodel Indian customs with a more encouraging result to point to as our aim than the England of the present day affords.

If a cup is full it is a truism to say that more cannot be poured in without some being spilt. And yet this is a problem—substituting countries and population—which all our legislators are bent upon solving. To what end? is the un-avoidable question. Is it truly thought better to rear 100,000,000 to poverty, famine, and vice, than to rear 50,000,000 who can live and find work and food? This seems to be the question, and the modern tendency is decidedly to say, 'Rear your 100,000,000,' and to add, 'and the Lord will provide'—knowing practically that the Lord, having made certain fixed laws as to food and population as well as to cups and water, will not interfere in the working out of these laws—not even to favour the most humane legislation.

Jan. 28.—This morning we have indulged ourselves with a prairie fire on a small scale, and found it very amusing. The wind being favourable, we set fire to the dry grass jungle between us and the water, and soon burnt about seven acres of it; indeed it is not out yet, so we cannot tell how much more will burn. It was quite exciting watching the long line of flame, leaping twelve feet high or more, as it seized greedily some specially tall thick piece of grass and spread with a loud sharp crackling like file-firing.

It improves the grass immensely for grazing, and would be done by the natives but that no Hindu will set it on fire on account of the insects he would destroy. I fear, indeed, the lives of many will lie at our door. The fly-catchers and a host of other birds had what an American would call 'a good time' catching the insects that were disturbed by the fire. We saw them darting through the smoke, and hovering round the ring of fire with the keenest interest; they did not seem the least afraid of it. We saw a kite swoop right down into the thickest smoke, but could not see if he got anything.

Two days ago the servants caught a crow, which I am taming. He already comes on to my hand and feeds without any shyness—indeed, crows are not burdened with shyness at any time. He has jesses on, and seldom now gets in a rage with them; he seems altogether philosophic, and bears his fate most patiently. The other crows come and sit by him sometimes, and are so sympathetic as to help themselves to his dinner in the most friendly way.

He was caught in such an ingenious way. A piece of meat was thrown down, to which a piece of string about fifteen inches long was tied, with a small stone at the other end. The crow seizes the meat and flies away with it, when the stone causes the string to swing round him and entangle him, bringing him to the ground, when he is quickly caught.

Feb. 7.—Here we are back again at Meerut, our pleasant camp life over for this season, perhaps over for ever, as when Robert is made Judge there is an end to camping.

There has been a good deal of trouble about the dhaie's child, which, since we left the station, has been brought to a very low ebb through neglect and immense doses of opium. So in spite of the parents I have dismissed the woman who had charge of it, and have at last found another who, I hope and think, will do well. She is now living here in the compound, that I may have the child under my own eye till we see it make a fair start again, poor little soul.

If it were a boy they would take enough care of it, but it is ' only a girl.'

I see the maximum and minimum marked by the thermometer in the house during our two months' absence has been 73°–53°. The house having been kept shut up, the range has been neither so high nor so low as if it had been thrown open.

Feb. 13.—We heard yesterday the terrible news of the disaster in Zululand, our loss having been altogether 1,100 men and 48 officers. Every one was horror-struck at the news ; but how true it is that events at a distance are seen as truly in perspective as objects are, and a dog dying at our feet will really affect us more than the news of an army being destroyed in the other hemisphere. In the evening a ball was given by the 9th Bengal Cavalry, and I do not suppose there was one absentee on account of the awful news just received.

Feb. 20.—Home from the Buffs' ball at two o'clock this morning, to find my voice weak and hoarse with having shouted to all my friends in my efforts to be heard above the band. Sitters-out would gladly have bands at double the distance and of half the strength.

The Buffs have magnificent plate, and their trophies were displayed on side-tables, mantel-pieces, and anywhere. The centrepiece last night, a splendid group standing two feet high, represented an incident in the Peninsular War, when an ensign stuck to the colours after his left arm was cut off. A lancer then rode at him, and cut him across the face, cutting his nose off, and he was found afterwards on the field, nearly dead, with the colours round him. He recovered, however, and I am told was the first person on whom the operation was ever performed of putting a false bridge to the nose and bringing down the skin of the forehead to cover it.

In a letter this week from Mr. Fitzgerald he tells us of his having entertained the Mahárája of Johore when he was lately in England. They had a big shooting luncheon, at which Johore ate fowl curry cooked by his own servants, but,

as Mr. Fitzgerald says, ' made of my poor cocks
and hens, which were taken off their nests,
throats cut, and left struggling about in a way
that brought tears into the cook's eyes!'

The address on the letter, to 'The Chief
Commissioner, Meerut,' made us laugh, as a good
illustration of how little people at home know
or care about titles and dignities in India. These
same dignities are so all-important to Indian
officials, more especially to those who have no
social position apart from their official one.
And then to think of this Visigoth at home con-
founding a Collector with a Chief Commissioner!
It is enough to give an Indian official a fit!

CHAPTER XVI.

HUSSARS' SKIRMISH—TROOPING THE COLOURS—SUNDAY OB-
SERVANCE — CONSERVATISM AND OBSTRUCTION — NAU
CHANDI FAIR—RIGOUR OF INDIAN GAOLS—SHAVING FOR
YOUR GRANDMOTHER—RIVAL PERFUMES OF HALF-CASTES
AND BRITISH SOLDIERS—DISASTER TO 10TH HUSSARS—
15TH HUSSARS RETURNED—INSECT CREATION—CHOLERA
BROKEN OUT.

Feb. 25.—The 15th Hussars have been
ordered home, and may be expected in two
months' time. The regiments at Kandahar appear to be nearly at starvation point; there is
next to no forage for the horses, and very little
water. The artillery horses were being shot
at the rate of two every day, and the Hussars
have lost a good many. As to the camels, it is
terrible to think of what they have suffered.
General Stuart's column alone has lost 900.

Affghánistán is a very difficult country to
invade. You dare not enter it with a small

force, and if you take a large one you are simply starved out for want of forage and water.

The Hussars had a brilliant little skirmish with some Affghán cavalry, and Major Luck was set upon by three Affgháns at once. He disposed of two, but got a tremendous blow on the sword-arm, which would certainly have taken it off but for the accident of his wearing that day a long-sleeved waistcoat, into the sleeve of which his wife had sewn a bit of chain. The chain was driven into the flesh, giving a severe bruise, but it saved the arm.

' Wednesday, March 5.—To-day is Mrs. ——'s garden party, and also service in church at six o'clock.

People are rather curious to see the result of this collision between the Church and the World —the more so as it is Col. —— of all people who has collided. He is our lay parson and churchwarden, and a strict church-goer. He always reads the lessons, and, when the chaplain is away, the whole service, with a little sermon at the end : this being the case, judge of the shock to everyone when he was heard to say to his wife at the church door last Sunday, after the chaplain had given out notice of service on Wednesday evening—' My dear, you must write and tell him he must put off the service on Wednesday ?'

As the General's wife says, ' If this is the shining light of the station, what is to be expected of us miserable sinners !'

Neither service nor garden party have been put off, so the collision is inevitable.

March 11, 10.30 A.M.—We have just returned from seeing the ceremony of trooping the colours of the Buffs, being the 307th anniversary of their being inspected by Queen Elizabeth. They were then called Trained Bands, and had no regimental number till after their return from Flanders, when the three regiments were numbered according to the order of their return, the Buffs thus coming to be third. Otherwise they are the oldest of all.

Trooping the colours is a pretty ceremony. I had never before seen any troops under arms since coming to India, as I never get up early, so it was quite a novelty to me. The parade began at 7.30, and was all over in an hour; after which we were invited to breakfast at the mess.

March 14.—We had our second garden party yesterday, and the glees we had been practising went really very well. Miss Planck sang a solo extremely well, interrupted, unfortunately, by a lively quarrel between two dogs in the verandah. It was very amusing to see every one who owned a dog get up with an anxious countenance and go out to see if it was *his* dog fighting.

A vigorous discussion is just now going on in the 'Pioneer' on the Sunday observance question, originated by its having published a long extract from an essay lately written by 'A Layman,' which has attracted some notice. Most of the correspondents' letters, however, are not worth reading, as they have failed to grasp the matter in question—viz., what the *authority* is for holding the observance of a seventh day to be binding on Christians. The weight of argument is at present too entirely on the Layman's side for the discussion to be called one at all, any more than a race between a Shetland pony and the Derby winner could be called a race. The pony's private opinion, however, if asked, would probably be that he had made a hard fight of it.

March 15.—To every one's surprise a really good letter appeared in yesterday's paper, signed by ' A Clergyman ; '—but in all points seconding the Layman's views, and enforcing his arguments.

This reminds me of a story Macaulay tells— of how at Cambridge a meeting was held, and a vote of censure on Wilberforce moved ; when up got Wilberforce and said, ' Mr. President, I beg to second the motion.'

This impartial *Padre* says he thinks that the Layman, and those who think with him, have far the best of the argument ; but he goes on to strengthen their case very ably. He quotes many of the Early Fathers and others. St. Cyril, Bishop of Jerusalem, A.D. 345, he says, writes :

' Turn thou not out of the way into Judaism, for Christ hath redeemed thee. *Henceforth reject all observance of Sabbaths.*' And St. Jerome says : ' On the Lord's day they went to church, and, returning, would apply themselves to their *allotted works, and make garments* for themselves and others.'

He observes that it is singular how the modern Sabbatarian views can have obtained in the Protestant Church, when we listen to Luther's and Knox's sayings. Luther writes : ' If anywhere the day is made holy for the mere day's sake—if anywhere any one sets up its observance on a Jewish foundation—then I order you to work on it, to ride on it, to feast on it, to do anything to remove this encroachment on Christian liberty.'

' As for Calvin,' the Clergyman goes on, ' I need only refer to the well-known fact that John Knox called on him one Sunday and found him playing bowls, to show that he had never heard of the sin of " Sabbath-breaking." Protestantism never did anything more mischievous than put-

ting the Ten Commandments of Moses into the
public service of the Christian Church. The
second commandment has no application whatever to Christians, and could have had very little
to the Jews. They are forbidden by it to "make
to themselves *any* graven image," yet carved
figures of cherubim were upon the walls and
door of the Temple, and were divinely ordered. . . .

'The old monks, who knew nothing about
Protestant Sabbatarianism, had a very good
proverb—*Laborare est orare*—Work is worship.
The man who does honest work on Sunday is
just as much worshipping as the man who goes
to church. The man who goes shooting on
Sunday, or plays cricket, or lawn-tennis, cannot
be said to be worshipping—but he is doing no
wrong, *and breaking no commandment.*'

This coming from a clergyman, although
only what is held by a great mass—perhaps the
great mass—of thinking laity (of course there
are many who neither have thought upon nor
studied the question, nor would do so) is very

unexpected. It is almost precisely what our
own chaplain allows—*vivâ voce*—that he holds ;
but he frankly admits that he has not the courage
requisite for martyrdom, and dare not preach his
views from the pulpit, or even in society where
he knows they would not be shared. He admits
that he is glad to see other braver spirits
throwing themselves into the breach, and
when he can safely pass in over their bodies he
will do so ! He said one day, when we asked
him why, holding these views, he did not boldly
preach them—' It is the accident of my profession. You have only to read history to see how
the Church has always been conservative and
always obstructive. I cannot free myself from
its influence—but some day we shall all be
dragged in a body from our present position, and
then I shall be able to speak where I now keep
silence.'

March 17.—We went yesterday to see the
Nau Chandi fair, held three miles from Meerut.
The booths were pitched along both sides of an
unmetalled road, and the sand was so deep that

the horses refused to drag the carriage any further. Luckily some elephants were there belonging to a native gentleman, and on one of them Mrs. Luck and I mounted ; it was quite a baby elephant, not more than seven feet high, and only room on him for us two and the mahout. Crowds of natives were there, all very quiet and orderly, and looking bright and gay in their white and scarlet holiday clothes. The stalls were filled chiefly with fruit, coarse pottery, tobacco, and hookahs, children's clay toys gaudily coloured, fans and lanterns of talc, sweetmeats, and such things. The pottery is extremely effective at a distance, and they have a fine turquoise blue, but it is very coarse when you see it near. Its coarseness is equalled by its cheapness, and for a penny you can buy a cup and bowl and plate ornamented very tastefully after a rude fashion.

Unfortunately, a dust-storm came on, scattering the people, and obliging the stall-keepers hurriedly to strike their tents. So we fled, bringing with us a hideous black toy bear, standing on his hind legs. The boy was quite afraid of the monster at first, but this morning is very fond of Bálu.

March 30.—This is a very good strawberry year. We have no strawberry beds, but buy ours from the gaol gardens. It sounds, per-. haps, strange to English ears hearing of gaol gardens, but a paternal Government here lightens the rigours of imprisonment by letting the prisoners work in the grounds belonging to the gaol—quite outside the walls. They go in gangs, each with irons on, certainly, and with a warder to look after each gang, but otherwise as free as ordinary labourers. Escapes are sometimes made, but not often. The prisoners are far too well off to be anxious to get away. One year at Fyzabad, during very heavy rain, the outer wall of the gaol began to fall, but the prisoners worked at it *con amore,* declaring with enthusiasm that though every other wall might fall, their gaol wall should not!

This promises to be a splendid year for mangoes. The trees are a mass of blossom, and the air heavy with their scent. There is a popular saying that ' A good mango year, a bad cholera year,' but I hope it may not be verified this year. Just now a great fair is going on at Hardwár, which is always watched rather anxiously, as it often proves a nursery for cholera, from which it is spread all over India as soon as the pilgrims begin to disperse.

On Friday the Rája of Bhurtpúr came here on his way to Hardwár, with twelve elephants, fifty horsemen, and a huge camp. We drove round to see his camp, and the road was crowded with streams of people, attracted by the fame of the Rája's grandeur.

Our bearer came to me lately with the information that his grandmother was dead. He did not profess sorrow, but, on the contrary, said that she was nearly a hundred years old, and that her death was a very good thing.

One thing, however, gave him anxiety, and he came to me that I might break it gradually to Robert. It was this. Custom required him, in sign of mourning, to shave all the hair on

his head and face; and he was so fully alive to the effect this would have on his personal beauty that he was most comically anxious for me to explain and apologize to his master. He seemed afraid of the shock it might cause him, should he not be duly prepared.

He certainly did look funny at first, and was very shy of showing himself. But now his glory -is returning.

March 31.—Maximum in shade, 102°; minimum ditto, 73°. To church yesterday evening as usual; but it is getting very hot, and I nearly had to leave in the middle of the service, chiefly by reason of there being a British soldier sitting between me and the wind. The combined perfumes of the half-castes and the soldiers make church absolutely unbearable to me as soon as the thermometer goes over 90°. I cannot breathe in it. Both are so dreadful that it is difficult to say which is worst; but the soldier at any rate does not ' go for to do it '—whereas if a person has ever so faint a tinge of native blood in his veins, it invariably prompts him to

scent himself (and still more *herself*) profusely
with the heaviest and most suffocating perfume
he can obtain—patchouli, sandalwood, otto of
roses, and such things. You can often smell
a carriage full of half-castes half a mile after
they have passed—in the hot weather, that is
to say, when the air is heavy and still. You
might run a drag after them with a pack of boys
for hounds.

April 5.—News came last night of a terrible
disaster at Jellálabad, when a squadron of the
10th Hussars was crossing the river, but missed
the ford, and forty-six men and one officer (a
cousin of Robert's) were swept away by the
current. No particulars are yet known, and it
seems strange that the fate of the leading men
should not have been able to save those behind
from sharing it.

April 14.—At church yesterday evening we
were sorely discomfited by the faithful puppy,
who contrived to give the syces the slip, and
came joyfully trotting up the aisle. He was
very good for some time, for he refrained from

speaking, and sat with one ear cocked and his eyes fixed on me with deep attention. But, alas ! his youthful restlessness presently moved him to go and inspect the choir, and he gave such contemptuous sniffs at them that there was imminent danger of his breaking into a bark, so Robert had to leave the church with him.

Robert is again officiating for three months as Judge. A heavy Sessions case is coming on to-day, in which Government is prosecuting a Treasury clerk who absconded years ago with public money. He was lately captured at Bagdad, and in a curious way. It seems that he wrote out a petition for some one there, and this petition by the merest accident came to the sight of a former Treasury officer here, who instantly recognized the writing. The clue was followed up, and the luckless wretch caught. Moral : Never write out anything for anybody if you have ever stolen anything !

April 25.—Maximum in shade, 112° ; minimum, 80° ; sun's rays, 171°. You see we have nice fine summer weather still. There is a great dread of cholera gaining ground. It is breaking out all over the country in the track of the pilgrims, and it appears to be of a very deadly kind.

It is now at Ambálla, and it will be a miracle if Meerut escapes. The poor Buffs! there will be a panic if it should break out among them; for when last they were quartered here they were twice-decimated by cholera, and left a fifth of their regiment in the cemetery here.

The first squadron of the 15th Hussars arrived yesterday. I have heard of men being 'darkened by the Indian sun,' but some of these are positively *blackened*. They are all very thin, but in excellent health. Unfortunately glanders has broken out among the horses since reaching India, and two had to be shot yesterday in the train—one of them the pony that has been carrying carpets Major Luck has brought from Kandahar. Poor beast! so near his labour's end, and then to lose his well-earned rest. Perhaps, however, he rests better as it is.

Major Luck has brought me two curious

Belooch shields as a souvenir of the war. One is of rhinoceros-hide, and is transparent like horn. The other is of common hide, studded over thickly with quaint brass knobs and ornaments. The Beloochis must be small men, or else have curiously small hands, for I can only just pass my hand through the straps at the back.

With the heat have also come, to my great solace, the water-melons. How they contrive to imbibe all the water they do is a mystery, planted as they are in deep burning sand, where a thistle would certainly refuse to grow, and where I think you might roast eggs with reason. Their nice pink flesh studded with black seeds is in itself refreshing to look at, and you can ladle out cups full of sweet watery juice, or juicy water.

May 1.—Yesterday evening I went for a drive, taking with me a lady only lately arrived. She is very young, and this is her first experience of India. At present her life is a burden to her by reason of the animal creation, as represented by wasps, lizards, crickets, and 'things with horns,' as she told me with a shudder. . These horned things are certainly startling ; they are enormous spiders with very long thick antennæ, and they glide about of an evening very swiftly. I always have them killed because of their likeness to scorpions, and for fear that a scorpion might some day pass muster as a spider. So the innocents are slain to make sure.

Poor woman ! when the rains come she will have toads to contend with, and 'creepand thinges' innumerable.

I have four friendly lizards who live in 'my bath-room, and are in no wise afraid of me. They are grown very fat, and I *hope* are fat with digested mosquitoes.

May 2.—We heard last night that cholera has broken out. Heaven send it may not spread. The last troop of the Hussars brought it, four men being taken ill immediately after their arrival here, of whom three died.

As we were driving on the Mall last evening we heard the three sharp crackling rolls which told us that another soldier's warfare was accomplished. How soon association of ideas invests anything with solemnity ! In itself there is nothing solemn in a volley of musketry, but through its associations the sound embodies all the solemnity of the Dead March.

It seems that there has been so much cholera on the railway that five or six dead bodies have been taken out from nearly every train arriving here. It is always kept very quiet, and we had heard nothing of it.

May 3.—Home letters to-day. What you say of L—— only shows to me that her nature is not in sympathy with ours, and no sense of duty can bring about sympathy ; it can only come from two natures being in tune with one another, and you sometimes find a person born with a nature pitched in a different key to those around him.

Some happy natures are pitched, as it were,

in an easy key, and find sympathy everywhere. Others, again, are in a difficult key, rarely met with ; but that is surely not a fault of theirs ? It is not the Æolian harp that tunes its own strings, but its Maker ; and it cannot sound until the right chord is touched.

CHAPTER XVII.

May 7.—I have been busy this morning
weighing out ounces of tea to be sewn up in bags,
and dyeing six dozen eggs scarlet, blue, yellow,
purple, and green. For this evening we have a
tea-party for all the waifs and strays we can
collect, and expect nearly sixty children—some
half-castes, and nearly all piebalds of varying
proportions. They belong to no regiment, and
are nobody's business in particular, so they
never get a treat of any kind.

The Scotch minister is my chief aide-de-camp, and is most kind and useful. When he came to talk over the arrangements he said, ' It is not to be denominational, I suppose ?' 'Certainly not,' quoth I. ' You even include '—he added doubtfully—' the Roman Catholics ?' I assured him poverty was to be the only passport, irrespective of creed. So we shall have what may be called ' a Christian mixture '—for I believe they will all be Christians of one kind or another ; queer ones some.

We are grieved to hear that the Hussars buried four more of their men yesterday who had died of cholera. Should another case occur, the whole regiment is to go into camp to-morrow. It is the only hope ; but at this time of the year, with the thermometer at 114° in the shade, the cure is nearly as bad as the evil.

May 8.—Our treat yesterday was a great success, and if eating may be taken as a gauge of enjoyment, the children enjoyed themselves thoroughly. The Easter eggs were a great pleasure, one little boy beginning to cry for fear all the scarlet ones should be gone before his turn came.

We had provided a merry-go-round and some first-rate jugglers. They performed the famous mango trick, which is always inexplicable, especially when performed as here on the bare ground, and with spectators in front and on all sides of the jugglers.· Then they put one of their people into a trance, and during the trance put a skewer through her tongue, and finally with great deliberation cut a piece off and handed it round for us to see. It certainly was flesh, and had we not known that we were there for the sole object of being imposed upon, we should have sworn it was a piece of her tongue, and that we had seen it cut off, and could still see her tongue hanging out and with the end gone.

How very little we can trust the evidence of our own senses ! and therefore how little it weighs with us when we hear a person say, 'But I *saw* it !' Yes, we reply; not for a moment do we doubt your honesty in saying that you saw it, but if we had seen it *ourselves* we should still not believe it, or rather believe that our senses had been cheated in the outrageous way we know they may be cheated.

The woman could not have had her tongue cut off and then healed; but if she had not, then we have no right ever to place the evidence of our eyes alone beyond contradiction.

When all was over, and it was quite dark, the minister made a little speech on behalf of the children. He was saying how much they had enjoyed the treat—'And whom have we to thank for all this?' One little boy promptly said 'The Lord;' but his remark falling flat the others saw his mistake, and chorussed 'Mr. and Mrs. King,' and cheered very heartily.

I paid rather heavily for venturing out earlier than I do on other days; for though I kept in complete shade, yet the air at 5.30 is like that of a furnace, and I got a smart touch of sunstroke. At the time I only felt my head queer, but at night such pain came on and such violent and prolonged sickness, that we quite thought I was in for cholera.

Warm wraps and mustard plaisters, however,

with iced cloths on my head, presently took
effect, and to-day I am nearly right again.

May 11.—Maximum, 113° ; minimum, 84° ;
humidity, 14°. Let me draw your attention to
the humidity of the atmosphere, which, as you
see, is 14° out of a possible 100°. Sometimes
it is lower ; on the 5th it was only 8°. This
represents a dry hot blast quite inconceivable
to any one who has not felt it.

In Bengal, Bombay, and Madras, they have
no idea of this. It is only experienced in the
Central and North-West parts of India.

I saw not long ago a report of the tempera-
tures of different parts of the world at certain
times of the year, and the North-West Provinces
of India are said to be the hottest part of the
whole globe during May and June.

Then they are partly compensated by having
a really bracing cold season, whereas the other
Presidencies have a monotonous climate all the
year round, never so fierce and never so invi-
gorating as it is here. People from Bengal
are perfectly amazed at the intense cold here at

Christmas, and are equally amazed at our fur-
nace-like atmosphere now——.

I often think our Christian resignation to
the divine will falls much below that shown by
these heathen and infidels. When the necessities
of life are at famine prices, and body and soul
have much ado to hold together, and rain is
needed to avert a general famine, and still the ·
sky continues white and merciless, you hear the
servants discussing its practical bearing on themselves with mournful head-shakings, but always
finishing with a patient sigh and the remark,
' But what can one say? it is God's pleasure.'

My old ayah was telling me the other day
of how her brother's son has gone with his regiment to this Cábul War, and hoping he will
return safe, as he is the only child left out of a
family of twelve. 'What!' I said, 'do you
mean that eleven have died?' ' Yes, all died.
Some at four, some at ten, and some older—but
none grew up. I don't know how it is God
left this one.' She said this with perfect
naïveté, as if it were a matter quite beyond her

understanding, and recognizing God's right to take them all.

May 16.—Carlie.[1] has begun to drink soup, and he has one quail jugged for him every day! It makes a small half-cup of most delicate broth, and he likes it much. We have nearly four hundred quail in our quail-house, and they are getting very plump now. They are witless birds, and accustomed to feed at daybreak. Men take advantage of both these facts to fatten them. They shut them up in a dark house underground, and twice a day let light in, when the quail feed greedily, not stopping to wonder at the frequent daybreaks.

May 17.—I have often heard of the advantages of setting a thief to catch a thief, but we have just shown our faith in the adage in an amusingly practical way. Robert as Judge loses the police guard he had as Collector, so the Judge has to hire a watchman or chokidár, to patrol round the house at night. It is not so much by his valour or vigilance that we profit, but that he, probably a rascal himself, is hostage

[1] Carleton, now ten months old.

for the good behaviour of his brother rascals. He generally takes life easily, and does most of his watching asleep. Our last chokidár, however, slept really too continuously, so we told the bearer to look out for another.

Now there is among men a caste called Gújars, who take so widely and kindly to thieving that it would be no great libel to call them a caste of thieves. The bearer sent off a trusty envoy to their headquarters to say that a sharp thief was wanted, and yesterday with great satisfaction he brought us a man who is, he assures us, fully qualified for the post of chokidár, and who is quite a king among thieves. What is more, Robert has taken him into our service!

This reminds me of an epitaph said to be in the churchyard at Peshawur, on the tomb of a missionary who was murdered by his chokidár :

Sacred to the Memory of the Rev. ——, &c.
He translated the Holy Scriptures into Pashtú,
and was shot by his own Chokidár.

———

'Well done, thou good and faithful servant.'

May 20.—Yesterday morning, after a succession of raging dust-storms, a slight shower of rain fell, and the sky was so overcast that it was actually possible to venture out of the house. So I strolled out with Robert to see how the garden looked by daylight. A bed of portulaccas was most brilliant. It was the first time I had seen them, as they are always shut up by the time I go out.

While we were loitering in the garden enjoying the unwonted scent of the rain on the thirsty earth, the puppy began dashing round a clump of tangled creeper, barking furiously. On Robert's going up to help him out rushed a jackal—a hideously mangy brute, nearly bald. The bearer remarked that his hair would grow again when the rain fell. I do not think natural history can be his forte.

May 28.—Robert has just accepted the offer of officiating for three months as Judge of Moradabad when his term of judgeship is over here in July. Moradabad is not more than eighty miles from here as the crow flies, and is on the other side of the Ganges. On looking it out in the 'Gazetteer' it is rather depressing to learn that 'scorpions and centipedes infest every building'—but somewhat consoling to be further assured that, 'though causing much suffering, they seldom produce death.' We at any rate know what we may reasonably expect—suffering, but probably not death.

June 2.—I have been busy all the morning grouping dried flowers for some lampshades promised for a bazaar. It is an excellent trial of patience doing it at this time of the year, and should be wholesome moral discipline. First of all the thermometer in this room is standing at 92°. Like all other things it seems to find much movement an exertion, so it only moves from 94° by day to 90° at night.

This in itself makes one irritable and impatient, so weak is our nature. Then the punkah keeps blowing away the dried flowers, and often, just as I had arranged a successful group, would come a specially vigorous waft of air and away the whole group would float.

Lastly a whole tribe of mosquitoes, black-striped, hungry, and ferocious, was hovering about me, and, ye gods! how I got bitten! being too much engrossed in my work to remember to stamp my feet, and wag my head, and flourish my hands. As group after group was completed, my ideas as to their value expanded, until I felt that none but a millionaire could adequately pay for the mosquito-bites and all the manifold trials embodied in those medallions of flowers!

June 4.—Last evening, when every one was driving on the Mall, a great brown cloud was seen in the north, and our hearts rejoiced to think a storm was coming. It advanced, however, so rapidly that it caught most of us unawares ; we looked up and saw its ragged brown edge ominously near, and in less than a minute the wind was howling and hissing round us, while we were enveloped in such complete darkness that we had to pull up. As soon as it got a little lighter Robert got down and walked in front of the horses until the thick brown darkness lifted sufficiently to make it safe to go at a trot again, when we made the best of our way home. We were of the earth, earthy, very, by the time we got there. Not a drop of rain fell, but still the air was cooled some degrees, and we had a refreshing night.

June 10.—We have heard this week of one of those rare romances in real life, the hero of which is a petty clerk in the Treasury here, getting a salary of 40*l.* a year. It seems that his father came out to India in the army as a private, and married here a half-caste woman. He died some time ago, since which the boy has been working in Government employ.

News has just come of his uncle's death in England, leaving property worth 3,000*l.* a year, which will be divided between this boy and another. I wonder how the change of fortune will practically affect him, and if he will go to England with his half-caste mother. Her colour would not be against her there as it is here—indeed would constitute her a *lionne* for society to run after. A half-caste is not without honour save in his own country.

June 12.—Last night we started after dinner to the other end of the station to see the circus of the 15th Hussars. The performance began nominally at gun-fire—viz. at 9.15—and as it was given under the tent of heaven the heat was never too oppressive, at least not to us spectators. It must have been exhausting work for the performers.

The circus was surprisingly good when you think that none of the men were professionals, and that just now they have been away seven months in Affghánistán, where neither men nor horses had circus training. All the usual circus feats were performed, riding two bare-backed horses, vaulting over the backs of six horses, and so on.

Then there was a dear little pony, most amusing and intelligent, who chased the clown whenever he saw him, making him vault out of the arena to escape. Any one was challenged to ride him, which challenge a private of the Buffs accepted, and was of course thrown off ignominiously every time he mounted, to the boundless pleasure of all the children present, who literally shrieked with delight at the pony's pranks.

A beautiful Arab horse, Robin Grey, was one of the features of the evening. He went through his tricks with great self-possession, and when at the end he stood quite still with his fore-feet on a high block, he looked round at the spectators with a proud expression in his full soft eyes, as if he really enjoyed their applause. He was a very dear beast, and was presented to the circus of the 15th by their last colonel.

On Tuesday evening we went to the cemetery. It was the first time I had seen it, and I was surprised at the extent of the City of the Dead. Its population must far outnumber that of the living.

Some of the graves date back fifty years, and you can very fairly guess their chronological order by noting their greater or lesser hideousness.

The favourite style forty years ago was a

mass of unmortared brickwork, whitewashed
and plastered outside, and in shape like a baker's
light van, without the wheels. Of these there
are hundreds and hundreds, one outdoing the
other in ugliness. Many of them are becoming
quite ruinous, the plaster having mouldered
away, disclosing the uncemented bricks, which
are tumbling down unchecked.

After this comes apparently the broken
column and pillar-post era, then an interlude of
obelisks, and then an imitation of Mahommedan
tombs, domed and columned, but vulgarized to
suit the taste of European undertakers. Some
of them are of immense size, symbolic of the
huge grief of the survivors, and you wonder at
such portentous sorrow being allowed room.

I am told there is now an order forbidding
the erection of any brick tombs, and it will effect
a great and much-needed reformation. The
modern part of the cemetery, with its simple
stone crosses, upright or horizontal, is quite a
relief to the eyes wearied with the monstrosities
of olden days. If the inhabitants of the old

tombs could awake and see their descendants lying under marble crosses, with in some instances the mystic letters R. I. P. on the tomb, they would shudder with pious horror to see how the Protestant world was losing its holy hatred of the Scarlet Woman.

Who can arise and prophesy what changes in taste and opinions another fifty years will work ? Opinions that now make our hair bristle, will they seem good to our grandchildren? Things we now cherish as beautiful, will they think outrageous?

So things go up, up, up, and so they go down, down, down. The only thing certain is that every dog will have his day, however ugly he may be.

CHAPTER XVIII.

HEAT INTENSE—THE WICKED ZULU—MOTHS IN THE PIANO—
HEAT APOPLEXY—RAINY SEASON—VANITY OF GLUE—AN
UNINTENTIONAL PRACTICAL JOKE—A FROG HANDICAPPED.

June 16.—The heat still intense. For the last week it has not gone below 90° in our bedroom at night. We keep the house jealously closed till 11 P.M., opening it then to let in a few hours of night air, and in this way we keep it from rising higher than 94° or 95°.

My morning sleep, the most refreshing of all, has lately been disturbed by the ants, who come up in numbers on to the bed and give me little sharp nips all over. When at last I wake, the bed is strewed with their dead bodies, as I kill them unconsciously when rubbing the bites. It is quite a new idea on their part, and hardly seems to answer well.

June 22.—Heard yesterday the sad news of the Prince Imperial having been slain by the Zulus. How little the savage who speared him could think that in giving him his death-blow he was also giving the death-blow to the hopes and ambitions of half France !

This Zulu War, as far as I can make out, is an unrighteous war—a war of aggression—and the Zulus are clearly in the right, morally, in defending their country against invaders.

The 'Saturday Review' quotes a couplet most appropriate just now, when speakers and writers are breathing slaughter against the wicked Zulu :—

> Cet animal est très-méchant,
> Quand on l'attaque il se défend !

What would be patriotism noble in an Englishman becomes bloodguiltiness intolerable in a Zulu. So do circumstances alter cases.

A piano-tuner came yesterday to put our piano to rights, and when the works were taken out a woeful revelation was made ! It was literally swarming with moths in all stages, and such havoc had they wrought in the cloth and felt that we are obliged to have it all put in new again. I have always kept the upper part carefully free from moths, and had camphor-bags ostentatiously strewn about. Meanwhile the moths crept in at the pedal-holes, and increased and multiplied undisturbed.

I am never tired of admiring our Indian flowers—indoors, for I see little of them out of doors. The máli's arrangements to-day are harmonies in pink and white ; and my Jaipúr elephants look perfectly lovely with their bowl piled up with sweet fresh pink roses, white petunias, large starry pink lilies, and the feathery graceful lagerströmia.

At home they will seldom be treated so magnificently—and yet how much more one *loves* home flowers ! For pure pleasure a bunch of primroses or cowslips surpasses the most brilliant and splendid bouquet of Indian flowers, and yet these are so lovely and pleasant to the eye that I feel ungrateful when I seem to slight them.

June 25.—We hear that the young fellow belonging to the Buffs who volunteered to ride the pony at the circus died two days afterwards of heat apoplexy. The regiment at Lucknow just out from home has lost seventeen men from it ; and at Muttra the Hussars had eight cases in one day only, of which four proved fatal.

It is not the sun that kills them—merely the heat of the air.

A week ago heavy rain fell, and our heat now is of the stewing order. Anything is better than the furnace blast ; and it is a relief being able to open the doors sometimes, after having so long been tightly shut up for eighteen hours out of the twenty-four.

The boy quite enjoys the extra liberty, and as soon as the doors are opened patters out into the verandah, having only to go on all-fours to cross the threshold, which in India is not sunk in the floor, but forms a bar three or four inches high across every doorway.

If their purpose be to trip up the unwary

and the old and the young, they certainly fulfil
it admirably.

There is one characteristic of an Indian hot
season, good or bad, according as you think.
Time simply flies, and before you are well into
a month you are out of it again.

It is owing to the absolute monotony. There
is nothing to look back upon, and nothing to
look forward to. One lives more absolutely in
the present than at any other time of one's life.
Sufficient unto the day is the evil thereof, and
the heat and the fatigue ; but as the next day
will be like unto it, and the next, and the next,
there is no particular desire to get it over, only
to make it as little wearying as may be.

So one eats one's breakfast leisurely, dawdles
over one's bath—the pleasantest time of all—
then reads, works, writes, without ever looking
out of doors, or even thinking of looking out of
doors, till the dusk shows it is time to venture
forth, and the servant announces that the carriage is round. Then a drive up and down the
Mall—the only watered road, therefore the *only*

road—home to a quiet dinner, and lo! the evening and the morning proclaim that another day
is gone.

July 4.—Maximum, 83°; minimum, 79°; humidity, 95°. We are having a splendid rainy
season ; not merely a succession of thunder-
storms as usual, but daily heavy soaking rain.
The thermometer is 30° lower than in May and
June, and mark, I pray you, the difference in
the humidity. It was then from 10° to 20° ;
now 95°.

We have to burn fires to dry mattresses,
books, and pillows, which begin to smell horribly
fusty. Gloves are all shut up in glass stoppered
bottles, and boots in air-tight tin boxes ; but
such things as cannot be shut up are suffering
from the generous humidity. The mouldings of
gilt picture frames are coming off in strips, and
the vanity of glue and cement is everywhere
being brought to light.

Just now I met with a ludicrous accident,
which might have turned out no laughing
matter. I was going to speak to the derzie,

who is working in the ante-room, and just as
I drew aside the *portière* and stepped out into
the hall, I stumbled, and fell flat with great
force. When I got up and discovered the cause
of my fall, I had to be very wrath to suppress
the tendency to laugh. The chuprassie, who is
·always in waiting, had laid himself down full
length on the deerskin at the door, and had
fallen asleep, never thinking of the consequence
to any one who should come out. It was a
mercy I had not the boy in my arms.

The man's contrition was so unmeasured and
abject that it made me still more inclined to
laugh. I bethought me of ' ye Chemiste,' when—

> Stumbling o'er the couchante page
> Liklakyng downe he went !

Only the page, unlike the chuprassie, had

> With a cunninge mal intente
> Couched him before the doore.

The effect, however, in both cases, was much
alike.

July 18.—We went yesterday to see the
weekly Gymkhána sports. The most amusing

thing was the Noah's Ark Stakes—among the entries for which were some bullocks, a frog, an elephant, several dogs, two turkeys, and a goat. It was of course a handicap, and as the frog was started within thirty yards of the winning post, public attention was for some minutes concentrated on him. He was accompanied and encouraged by his trainer, an officer in the Buffs, and an erratic charge he proved. He hopped with zeal, but not always in the right direction, and, besides losing the race himself, caused all the dogs to lose it, as they were too much interested in so remarkable a rival to run any further themselves.

CHAPTER XIX.

JOURNEY TO MORADABAD—LOCUSTS—GENESIS OF BUTTERFLIES
—DISASTROUS FLOOD—THE FATE OF PIONEERS—UPHILL
STRUGGLES—CAN CREEPING PLANTS SEE?—COMBAT WITH
A RAT.

Moradabad, July 22.—We left Meerut by
the mail train on Sunday morning, and on our
way here passed through a large flight of locusts.
When we came up with the advance guard, the
train stirred up a thick cloud of those that had
lighted on the ground. The engine divided
them as a boat-keel does the water, and a dense
cloud streamed away like smoke on either side
of it. It must have been a very extensive
swarm, as we did not lose sight of it for some
hours, owing to the turns the railway takes,
and to the pace at which the locusts were
moving.

In many of the fields we saw the distracted

owners with their sons, and cousins, and fathers, and uncles dashing frantically about, waving all their available garments in wild efforts to make the locusts move on, at least to their neighbour's field. In others, they seemed to be looking on in helpless despair. Poor things! What with drought, flood, and locusts, a farmer's couch cannot be of roses.

Compared with Meerut this seems quite an out-station. There are only four ladies here at present, and no troops except one detachment of the 2nd Regiment.

We took a drive yesterday evening, the most remarkable thing we saw being some ruinous though unfinished barracks, which had been built up half-way, at an enormous cost, and then abandoned. Government will need to save many pence, and cut down many a petty clerk's salary, before it makes good the lacs of rupees thrown away here.

July 26.—The house we are in belongs to the former Judge here, and has a good garden, with a lawn quite English-looking. Yesterday

Watering
the Garden – Ambálla
Nov. 30.

was a very cloudy day, and as I sat with the windows open (for in this house there are windows which are not doors, a thing somewhat uncommon), and heard the sound of the mowing machine, I could almost fancy we were in England.

The birds, too, take to chirping and singing in this rainy weather, whereas they are absolutely silent in the hot season.

Yesterday we found a very large caterpillar in the verandah, and, being curious to see what butterfly it belongs to, have shut it up in a cardboard box, in the hope of its living and turning into a chrysalis. None of the servants, apparently, had ever heard that there was any connection between caterpillars and butterflies, and consequently, in spite of their respect for me, their disbelief was very evident when I explained to them that all butterflies came from caterpillars.

One of the chuprassies, indeed, by way of supporting me and yet adhering to probabilities, said, ' Yes, verily, this beast will lay eggs, and from them shall butterflies be hatched!' But when I declined this testimony, he too went over to the ranks of the unbelievers.

Aug. 2.—Alas for the cause of science and education! The caterpillar is dead, and with him all hope of proving to our servants the truth of what we told them concerning the mysteries of Nature.

The rain it raineth every day, and when it does not the atmosphere gives one a good idea of what the inside of a Warren's cooking-pot would be.

In the midst of all this steaming heat we have but to raise our eyes to the north, and there we see a jagged range of hills, and we know that there—only fifty miles distant—is a climate as cool as France, where people can enjoy a fire of an evening.

The sharpness of the contrast ought to make one feel discontented, but I do not think it does. Our principal feeling is one of gladness that the hills are so near, and that in case of necessity so short a flight would take us out of the heat.

The very thought makes us better able to bear what we have to go through, for it takes away its element of hopelessness.

Aug. 4.—The river here, the Rám Ganga, is in flood, and rose yesterday two feet above the highest known flood-mark. Miles of country are under water, and fifteen villages drowned out. The engineers and a detachment of the troops were busy all yesterday trying to save the unhappy villagers, who had taken refuge on the roofs of their huts—a very frail and brief refuge, for the walls are rarely more than five feet high, and, being built only of mud, collapse very quickly when in the water.

Rafts were made, and the rescuing party worked all day, but many lives were lost. Cattle were washed away in great numbers, few, indeed, being saved.

Such an unprecedented flood caused great excitement, and crowds flocked to the river's edge and swarmed on all housetops that commanded a good view of the floods.

The river was like a small sea, its thick

yellow water rushing and eddying along with a fine sound. There must have been a very heavy fall of rain in the hills to produce this sudden and disastrous rise.

Aug. 5.—I have been reading some of Sydney Smith's writings, and very full of practical sense and clear sight they are. His views on the public school system, female education, and other such matters were a good half-century in advance of his time, so it was natural that he should earn thereby the suspicion and dislike of his contemporaries. There is something sad in seeing a man urged on, against all his worldly interests, by some powerful voice within him, fighting against the whole tone and feeling of his age, and knowing that had he lived fifty years later he would have had no need to fight at all, or that the very opinions for which he was detested and persecuted have now been adopted by the slow-moving masses.

It is, however, always the fate of those who lead opinion, and, 'like the more delicate barometers, foretell a change when their slower com-

panion instruments can as yet see none coming.'
The masses really move at the same pace as
their leaders, but nearly a century behind them.
Is it not strange that they never learn from past
experience that the liberal spirits in the van are
not really wicked or revolutionary, but are
merely standing now where fifty or a hundred
years hence they will themselves stand ?

We now acquiesce so completely in the
political and civil emancipation of Jews and
Roman Catholics, and in the abolition of torture
for witchcraft, and look upon the present state
of thought regarding such matters so completely
as the natural common-sense one, that we can
hardly realize to ourselves the time—not so
very long ago—when the few bold spirits whose
crime was to think *then* as the rest of the world
does *now* did so at their peril, and were called
dangerous, irreligious, freethinkers, infidels, and
were feared and shunned by the conservative
orthodox party.

We have only to read history to find that
every advance in religion, science, or morality

has been alike made at the cost of its leaders, and in the teeth of the bitter opposition of the masses. Still we do not profit by this knowledge, but cry out as eagerly as of old to stifle those who promulgate new ideas not in accordance with our present ones.

I fancy there are movements now on foot, and being met with violent wrathful opposition, which will appear in much the same light as the Catholic emancipation to our grandchildren, who will be amazed to read of the uphill fight it once cost to carry them.

Aug. 7.—The mango season is almost over, to my deep regret! Robert has made the alarming calculation that I have eaten thirteen stone weight of mangoes in two months! It is always said that you get boils if you eat too many mangoes, according to which I have certainly not eaten too many. It is always well to be temperate.

Robert has broached a theory that I cannot remember to have met with before—viz., that creeping plants can *see*, or at any rate have some

faculty equalling sight.   He was sitting in the
verandah with one foot up against a large pillar,
near to which grows a kind of convolvulus.
Its tendrils were leaning over into the verandah,
and to Robert's surprise he presently noticed that
they were visibly turning towards his leg.   He
remained in the same position, and in less than
an hour the tendrils had laid themselves over
his leg.   This was in the early morning, and
when at breakfast he told me of this discovery
we determined to make further experiments.
When we went out into the verandah the tendrils
had turned their heads back to the railing in
disgust.   We got a pole and leant it up against
the pillar, quite twelve inches from the nearest
sprays of convolvulus.   In ten minutes they had
begun to curve themselves in that direction, and
acted exactly as you might fancy a very slow
snake would do if he wished to reach anything.
The upper tendrils bent down and the side ones
curved themselves until they touched the pole,
and in a few hours were twisted quite round it.
It was on the side away from the light, and,

excepting the faculty of sight, we can think of
no other means by which the tendrils could be
aware that the pole had been placed there.
They had to turn away from the light to reach
it, and they set themselves in motion visibly
within a few minutes of the pole's being there.

We have had heavy and continued rain, and
at Naini Tál they have had 115 inches in three
months. I think in England it takes a year's
rain to make up 40 or 50 inches; so you can
imagine what kind of rain is required to bring
115 inches in 90 days. It is a pity Noah kept
no rain-gauge.

This morning a great big rat, a bandicoot,
was killed here, and brought in triumph by the
valiant bearer, who had slain him in single combat with a sharp spit, and says he growled like
a dog. We measured it, and found it was
twenty-two and a half inches from nose to tip of
tail—of which about half was tail.

Sept. 8.—Another awful tragedy to mark
this year ! We have just heard the news of Sir
Louis Cavagnári and the whole of the English

guard at Cábul having been massacred. The telegram is frightful in its brevity, for we know no particulars beyond that the native regiments rose and the mob joined them. An immediate march on Cábul is ordered from Jellálabad and the Kurram.

And this is the amen to all the songs of peace and triumph that have been sung with such self-satisfaction by all the diplomatists lately ! Cábul will indeed have cause to be remembered by Englishmen, for this disaster seems to be as complete—though not so vast—as the one in 1841.

CHAPTER XX.

RÁMPÚR—HINDUSTANI MUSIC—A TWO-STORIED CARRIAGE—
BAMBOO FORTIFICATIONS—A SNAKE HUNT—SUPPRESSIO
VERI—FEVER RAGING—NINETY PER CENT. OF POPULATION
ILL—OUR CHURCH-BELL—A FIGHT WITH AN EARWIG.

Rámpúr, Sept. 20.—I am writing this from
Rámpúr, where we have been the Nawáb's
guests since yesterday. It is only eighteen
miles from Moradabad, and on hearing that we
wished to see his city, the Nawáb wrote to
invite us there, and promised to send a carriage
and make all arrangements. We drove in our
own carriage down to the river, and then crossed
in the ferry-boat. The river has fallen nearly
as rapidly as it rose, and the crossing is now
only a matter of ten minutes, but when it was
in flood it destroyed more than a mile of the
road on the other side, so that carriages cannot
be brought to meet the boat.

An elephant was therefore waiting for us, and took us across the stretch of flat muddy land from which the water has lately retreated, to where the Nawáb's carriage was standing, drawn by four mules. They were strong hardy beasts nearly fourteen hands high, and they had no too easy work, for besides ourselves there was the coachman and our own two servants on the box (Heaven only knows where they put their legs, for all our bags and bundles were packed up in front), and three men hanging on behind. One of the leaders was ridden by a postilion, and away we dashed at a gallop of fifteen miles an hour, which we kept up the whole way, changing mules twice, and finally having a team of horses, bright spirited chestnuts, which took us clattering into the city. Wonderful to say, we ran over nobody, not even a dog, but it was not our fault.

At the palace we were met by General Azím-u-dín, a fine portly man in uniform, who speaks English excellently.

The Nawáb is a great invalid, and rarely

shows.   He came over this morning from his part of the palace and had an interview with Robert, but it was before I left my room, so I have not seen him.   I hear he looks very ill, and has to be supported as he walks.   He is a perfectly independent prince, and keeps up a little army on the scale of the German princelings and grand dukes.

We have been entertained since coming here by a succession of shows of various kinds—fencers, jugglers, actors, musicians, and painters have all shown us their skill.   The Hindu music quite passes my comprehension.   I have heard that great European musicians consider it very beautiful and interesting, and highly scientific, and I have listened with attention and patience to performers who are considered masters of the art, but my candid opinion (given at the risk of writing myself down a Goth) is that it is the most tuneless, head-splitting, hopeless, endless jangle.   I can find no harmonies, no theme, no tenderness, no meaning.

If it is accompanied by singing, the words

are articulated very rapidly, with innumerable little quirks and twirls, and apparently no attempt at giving any expression. If it is beautiful, its beauty is too high for me ; I cannot attain to it. I will risk no more headaches in the hope of some day seeing the beauty of Indian music as performed by native musicians.

Their fondness for their abominable drum or tom-tom shows in itself a different idea of music to mine. I could not think 'Robin Adair' or Beethoven's Andante improved by the perfectly monotonous accompaniment of a very toneless drum. These people delight in it, and no singing or acting can go on without it. My head ached for hours last night after the musical performance, though we cut it almost ungraciously short.

This morning we were taken to see the Nawáb's stables. As in most native establishments, there is no attempt at making the stables themselves handsome ; they are merely long irregular rows of tiled sheds in more or less disrepair, and the countless stable servants about the place are all as dirty and ragged as it seems good to them to be—as strong a contrast to the stables and servants of an English gentleman as could be seen. But the Nawáb had some good horses. About fifty were led past for our inspection, chiefly Arabs, the rest Australian or Rámpúr bred.

Besides these he has twenty-five mules, and as neither he nor his son ride, and seldom drive either, the animals eat the corn of idleness, except when he sends out to meet any guests.

The most curious thing we saw was a *two-storied* carriage, about seventeen feet high ; it was built after the Nawáb's own design, and was intended to be used when he drives to his summer palace.

This palace is only three miles distant, but for fear of being bored during the transit he had this carriage built big enough to allow of a nautch being performed inside. The upper storey, to which you mount by wooden steps, is for the servants' accommodation.

This Noah's Ark, or Juggernaut's Car, is

drawn by sixteen horses, four abreast, and the weight of it must be about three tons.

We then drove to see the summer palace, though our way was not beguiled by any nautch. There were many very ancient, and I dare say rare, prints of various Durbars in olden days, and of Wellesley, Lord Minto, and other famous Indian names. The General pointed out to us particularly a print of Landseer's 'Sanctuary,' old and stained with damp, not a proof, and which must have cost a few shillings originally. He assured us it was very valuable. The native taste in pictures is not of a high order ; every room was hung with gaudy French prints of women in full dress—viz., with very little dress at all—and in general they are hung in *pairs*, so that if there are eight pictures, four of them are duplicates.

The sun was very powerful, and I dared not stay out longer, so we returned to the palace, and the Nawáb's painter was summoned. His painting is what we call illumination and writing, and is extremely beautiful and graceful. He is

now engaged in illuminating a book compiled by
the Nawáb, and it will be of great value. The
fineness of the work was such that in one instance
a toothed-line border which I immediately
noticed was hardly visible to Robert, who took
it for an ordinary line. The man was delighted
at my appreciating it, and observed to the
General that I was 'a very good looker.' He
has promised to do me a specimen page, which
I shall prize greatly. In the primitiveness of
his implements, colours, and materials, he re-
sembles one of the old monks in the days when
Winsor and Newton were not. His brushes
come from squirrels born and bred in the
Rámpúr groves, and are mounted on quills
from the fretful porcupine. His gold leaf he
beats out himself from a gold mohur. His
colours he grinds and mixes as though 'moist
colours' had not as yet burst upon the world.
He probably never heard of them.

There is nothing much to see at Rámpúr;
the city is quite modern, and has no history or
associations. Its one beauty is its fortified wall,

surrounding the city in a ring of nine miles, unbroken save for twelve gates. And this wall is of
bamboos—living, growing, feathering bamboos,
in a dense tangled belt, sometimes sixty feet
high, and totally impassable except to pigs and
jackals. Once in ten years it is cut down, and
the General says that hundreds of wild pigs are
then turned out. One boar rushed into the city
and killed seven people before it could be shot.

We started on our drive homeward at four
o'clock, reaching Moradabad in little over two
hours.

Sept. 26.—A great excitement to-day in the
form of a snake hunt. As we were sitting at
luncheon the bearer came in to report that a
large cobra had been seen to climb up into a
bushy creeper, and would we give the order to
have him turned out. By all means, said
Robert, not loving cobras; and, being a cloudy
day, we went out to see the result. The creeper
he had taken refuge in was a very thick one,
growing up a wire frame about eighteen feet
high, and when we arrived was surrounded by

an eager crowd of servants armed with poles and sticks. If might is right, the poor cobra was very much in the wrong.

The men soon stripped away part of the creeper, and then the snake was espied at the very top. Before long he found his position untenable and dropped suddenly down, when he was speedily beaten to death amidst great excitement and exultation. He was a fairly big cobra, rather over four feet long.

Sept. 30.—September is quite keeping up its character for being the most feverish month in the year. Numbers of our servants are down with fever, and the mortality from it just now is excessive.

It is very hard to know how to treat these native servants, for they have all the foolishness of children and yet have the independence of men. Their foolishness makes them refuse quinine because it is nasty, and their independence prevents one's *forcing* them to take medicine as one would a foolish child.

By the doctor's orders, however, I now insist

on their all taking daily two doses of a prescription he has given me, and which I make up myself, carefully using only new vessels of native pottery, so that no objection can be made on that score. Then at stated hours the servants appear, each with his own brass cup, into which I pour the dose and see it drunk in my presence.

The prescription includes quinine, chiretta, lemon-juice, and *rum*, and this morning I was obliged to connive at an untruth concerning it. The servants, knowing it was a prescription of the Doctor Sahib's, and was therefore *medicine*, had made no troublesome inquiries, and had all swallowed their dose till the turn of a certain Brahmin punkah-coolie came. He came obedient to the command, and with gratitude and salaams received his jorum, with which he was then departing with the pious intention of throwing it into the nearest bush. On my telling him to drink it at once he looked round in an appealing way and said, ' But is it certain there is no sharáb [spirit] in it ? because you all know I am a Brahmin.' I kept silence, but a chorus arose to assure him the dose was innocent, 'was it not the Doctor Sahib's own prescription ? ' So he drank it, and I trust may never be the worse for it here or hereafter, nor I for my silence.

Oct. 3.—This fever is like a plague ; nearly all work is at a standstill. Robert is holding the Sessions here this week, and can hardly get through it at all. His decree-writer has just died after three days' fever ; the Government prosecutor and half the other officials are down with it ; and this morning three more have sent in petitions saying they are too ill to attend. The Police Magistrate says almost all his men are down with fever, and the thieves would have a good time of it if they too were not laid low. The Engineer (who is himself very ill with fever) has had orders to get the Naini Tâl road in order by the 10th, and is at his wits' end to know what to do, as nearly all his staff are *hors de combat.*

It is so raging in the city that the native medicines are exhausted and the Hakíms so worn out that they have shut their doors and refuse to stir.   I send for a tailor who has worked for me, but he cannot come, being ill with fever. I send to a shop for things wanted, but the shop is shut up, all being down with fever.   I write to the postmaster about a parcel miscarried, but he is too ill to attend.

Oct. 7.—The accounts that come in from all sides respecting the ravages made by fever are terrible.   In the Aligurh District the mortality has been so great that the villagers now, instead of burning or burying their dead, are throwing them into the drainage-cuts along the railway, and numbers of corpses are to be seen as you go down the line.   The Assistant Magistrate here told Robert yesterday that he had not had a case to try for seven days, both prisoners and witnesses being down with fever.

Only yesterday, when Robert was trying a Sessions case, one of the witnesses died suddenly in the verandah of the Kutcherry, from exhaustion caused by fever.   He was a policeman, poor fellow, and the fatigue of coming in six miles from his village had been too much for him.

No one seemed aware he was sick unto death, and he died in the midst of the people about the Court as quietly as if he had indeed only fallen asleep.

A correspondent of the ' Pioneer ' writes from Pertábghur to say that fully ninety per cent. of the population are suffering from fever ; field work is almost suspended, and in many homes one and all are prostrate. From Meerut we hear that twenty thousand deaths were registered in September, being about 16,000 in excess of the monthly average.

I have been myself just laid up for three days, and when I first got up could hardly walk straight, being so ridiculously weakened by the fever. A few hours of it seem to take all strength out of one.

Oct. 12.—To-night we shall have the fortnightly light of our chaplain's countenance shed upon us. I must send you a sketch of our church-bell, as it is somewhat different from an English one. The bell is a plain metal disc, hung from a tripod of bamboos, and its clapper is the mild Hindu. Some of these bells have a very fine deep tone, but this particular one is rather cracked in tone. So indeed is our chaplain, poor man, who is so asthmatic that it is painful to hear him gasp out the service.

Oct. 14.—I always thought earwigs were loathsome beasts, but never knew how much cause the insect world has for sharing my opinion. Last night there was a fine and varied collection of insects on my mantelshelf, attracted by the lamp, and among them I noticed a gigantic earwig, armed with the largest forceps I ever saw.

In order to stop his wanderings I turned a tumbler over him, enclosing also a cricket about his own size, and a flying bug which looks like a small beetle, but if touched emits a smell so horrible that you loathe yourself for the next half-hour.

These three seemed perfectly indifferent to each other, the cricket calmly drawing each of his antennæ in turn through his mouth, and the bug spending most of his time in tumbling on to his back and then struggling to right him-self.

I now think that the cricket's apparent calmness was assumed to conceal his deadly fear, for I suppose he knew earwigs better than I did.

In the morning a great tragedy had occurred. The poor cricket's head, body, and tail were severed from each other, and remains only of his legs were to be seen, while of that unsavoury bug nought remained but the horny wing-covers. The earwig had lost one of his antennæ, and in spite of his victories and banquet did not seem very lively. The bug had revenged himself.

We were up at daybreak this morning to start off the boy and his suite to Meerut, where he is to stay with some friends of ours for ten days, while we take a scrambling trip to Naini Tâl. Heigh-ho for the hills!

END OF THE FIRST VOLUME.

G. & C.

Spottiswoode & Co., Printers, New-street Square, London.

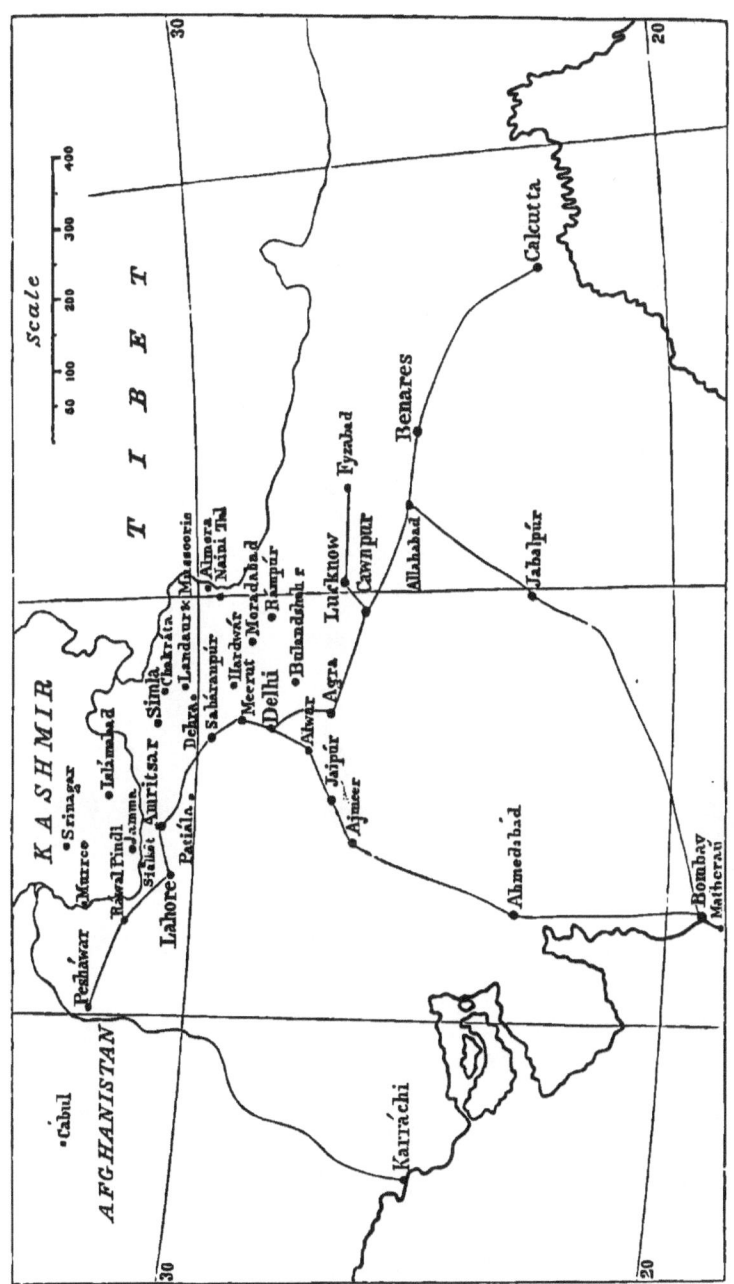

www.ingramcontent.com/pod-product-compliance
Lightning Source LLC
Chambersburg PA
CBHW020947030726
47496CB00005B/1388